# RESCUED BY THE HERO

## HEROES OF FREEDOM RIDGE

### MANDI BLAKE

Published in the United States of America
Cover Designer: Amanda Walker PA & Design Services
Editor: Editing Done Write
Ebook ISBN: 978-1-953372-01-7
Paperback ISBN: 978-1-953372-02-4

# CONTENTS

*To Tara Grace Ericson and Hannah Jo Abbott, whose friendship has been a wonderful blessing.*

Greater love has no one than this, that someone lay down his life for his friends.

— JOHN 15:13 (ESV)

# 1

*J*oanna Drake finished typing the last line of notes to her boss before interrupting the associate attorney chattering on in her office. "Keith."

Her tone was bold, stopping him mid-sentence. Should she be so blunt with him? He was her superior, as far as the firm hierarchy was concerned.

Forget it. She needed to put her foot down now or he would continue to bother her.

Joanna waited a heartbeat to make sure she had his full attention and eye contact before continuing. There was no way he hadn't understood her the first time—or the fifteenth time. "I believe I already said no. I'm not changing my mind."

Keith settled back into the chair across from her desk with a huff. "Come on. It's just one date."

She focused on controlling her rising temper and moved her attention back to the screen. She'd been warding off Keith Sanders' date requests for weeks now, and his advances had become annoying. The guy needed to move on. Thankfully, he wasn't her boss, and she only saw him around the office occasionally. She worked in the estate planning division, while Keith was a real estate attorney with an office on a different floor.

"I just want to show you a good time."

As if she would be interested in any good time with the creep of the firm. Keith had been hanging around her office too much lately. He chatted a lot, but she rarely remembered anything he said. She'd become a champ at tuning him out.

Definitely not her type.

Joanna counted backward from five before responding.

"I'm not in the mood for a good time right now. I'm leaving in less than ten minutes, and I won't be back until after the new year."

Her boss, Duncan Crosby, was a kind man who always took the month of December off when the courts cleared their dockets. This year, he'd extended the same benefit to her. She hadn't taken a single day off since she began working for him two years ago. She'd agreed to keep in touch through email and calls from her cell on occasion, and she was ready to go.

Keith grinned, but the expression didn't exude joy. "Where are you going?"

"I'm spending the holiday with my brother."

"Where?" he questioned again.

Did he possess any tact? There was no way she would be telling creepy Keith where she was going. "Out of town." She tilted her head and gave him a close-lipped grin that dared him to press her further.

"What about when you get back?" He leaned forward with that mischievous grin as if he'd found a loophole.

Joanna shoved a file into her bag and huffed an exasperated sigh. "Don't you have work to do?"

He crossed his ankle over a knee, dangling his pristine wingtip shoe. The sharp suit wasn't enough to turn her eye when he wiggled his brow at her. "Nothing more important than convincing you to go on this date with me."

She was going to barf. The man had zero charm and a whole lot of misplaced confidence. Keith might actually be handsome if he wasn't such a screw up. His frame was lean and toned, his hair was always well groomed, and his suits fit him like a model. Not to mention his light-brown hair and blue eyes gave him a friendly face.

However, Joanna could easily look past his symmetrical features and see the pushy, lazy attitude that held no compatibility with her own.

Her phone chimed with a message. It was her brother.

Zach: I'm here.

"Listen, Keith, I have to go." She slung her bag over her shoulder and clicked the last buttons to shut down her laptop.

"Last chance," he taunted.

Joanna shoved her laptop and charger into her bag. "For the last time, I'm not interested." Those words would undoubtedly fall on deaf ears. He hadn't been listening to her for weeks.

Keith stood as she rounded the desk and made her way

through her small office. His fingers encircled her upper arm as she passed, and she turned to him with a glare.

He sputtered, "But—"

"But, I should get going," Joanna interrupted, jerking her arm from his grasp. "I'll see you after the new year." She stood at the door, waiting for him to exit first so she could lock up.

Finally, Keith left with a grumbled, "See you later."

Joanna locked the door, and Keith wasn't anywhere to be found when she punched the elevator call button. It would be a long month before she stepped foot back through the doors of Miller and Baker. She'd been at the law firm for two years now, and as much as she liked her job, a holiday getaway was much needed.

The elevator opened on her floor, and a woman she'd never seen before stepped in with her. The young woman was pretty and looked sweet. Was Keith harassing her for a date too?

Joanna wasn't one to complain unless warranted, but perhaps it was time to have a talk with the HR department about Keith's behavior, or at least her boss. Although he hadn't actually done anything wrong beyond annoying her and wasting time in her office during working hours, she still felt icky when he was around.

Stepping out of the high-rise where she worked and onto the sidewalk of downtown Phoenix, Joanna soaked up the sun's warmth. Soon, she would be bundled in sweaters and layers in Freedom, Colorado. She'd only been to the Rockies to visit Zach a couple of times when he'd been in college, and he made it sound like the perfect place to spend Christmas.

Their parents would be spending the holiday with her brother, David, and his family in Texas this year. Joanna and Zach both insisted they were adults who could handle one Christmas away from home, but their parents had still been reluctant to leave two of their children out for the holidays. The trip to Freedom was a way of letting their parents know they would be having a great time.

She tapped out a text letting Zach know she was outside, and his car pulled up to the curb within seconds.

Joanna slid into the passenger seat. "Someone is ready to hit the road."

"You better believe it." Zach merged back into traffic. "The slopes are calling my name."

Joanna stashed her purse and laptop bag in the back seat and turned back around to face the busy street ahead. "What am I supposed to do while you're out skiing all day?" she asked.

"Snowboarding. I'll be snowboarding. There's a difference."

Joanna raised her hands in surrender. "Excuse my ignorance. You spent a couple of winters in Colorado, and suddenly you're a pro."

"I'm pretty good at it."

"Anyway, my question still stands. What am I supposed to do?" She didn't want to be stuck in a hotel room for a month, and she didn't see herself as a snowboarder.

Zach brushed a hand through his dark hair that was a stark contrast to her blonde. It had gotten considerably longer since she'd seen him last month. "Aiden said there's lots of stuff to do at the resort."

"Aiden?" she asked as she flipped open the visor mirror and lifted her hair into a ponytail.

"My roommate from college. You remember him. You met him a few times."

"Oh," Joanna let the sound linger on her rounded lips. "*That* Aiden."

Of course, she remembered Aiden Clark. Her brother's tall, dark, and handsome best friend from college had been hard to miss. It had been a few years since she'd seen him, but Aiden had been her crush in high school. He was charming, funny, playful, and outgoing.

In short, he was everything she wasn't.

Perhaps that had been the root of her attraction. He was adventurous and bold, not to mention her brother had explicitly made sure she knew Aiden was off-limits from day one.

"Yeah, he works at the resort."

He officially had her attention. "At the Freedom Ridge Resort? So, he'll be there?" She tried to keep the curiosity from her tone.

"Of course. He told me there are lots of Christmas activities and things to do. Don't worry."

Surely she could find things to do to fill her days, but a month's worth of days? Maybe she should grab a book or two at her apartment before they left town. With Zach spending most of his time with Aiden, she didn't want to spend the entire vacation alone.

She refused to let her fun-filled Christmas vacation turn into a bore fest before she even arrived at the resort. This holiday wouldn't be spent at home with her family, but she was determined to have some fun.

## 2

*A*iden slapped his student on the back as they made their way in from the slopes. "I'm telling you, you're a natural."

"Really?" Bruce was barely fifteen and still bouncing on his toes from their first lesson.

"You picked it up easy today. Just keep working on that balance. Practice in your cabin tonight, but don't fall off of anything." Aiden stressed the last part as he rubbed the back of his head. He'd learned that lesson after trying to balance on the side of the bathtub. "Trust me. Keep it low to the ground."

Bruce nodded. "Got it, boss. Heel toe."

Aiden playfully bumped the boy's shoulder with his fist. "It's that simple, if you can believe it."

The warmth of the lodge settled over him as they stepped inside. He loved the contrast of the adrenaline and body heat against the frigid air of the Rockies in the winter, but coming back to his home base was a comfort like no other. When that heat hit his bones, his entire body melted.

"Thanks again. Catch you Thursday." Bruce waved as he ran off to Mountain Mugs, the coffee bar at the Freedom Ridge lodge that was second to none.

Aiden shoved his beanie and gloves into a cargo pocket of his pants and removed his phone from another. Three messages waited, all from his friend, Zach.

Zach: We're here.

Zach: Meet you at Mountain Mugs.

Zach: Forgot to tell you Joanna was coming.

Joanna? Did Zach bring a girlfriend on vacation? Aiden hadn't known his friend was seeing anyone, much less in a relationship that was serious enough for a month away together. What happened to their month of snowboarding? So much for the bro code.

Aiden lengthened his stride when he spotted his friend scanning the lounge. Zach had visited Freedom Ridge the year before last, but the coffee shop he owned in Phoenix was growing and requiring more of his time.

Zach spotted Aiden, and they greeted each other with a solid handshake and a slap on the shoulder.

"Glad you could make it," Aiden said.

"I wouldn't miss it," Zach replied. "You finished for the day?"

"Just wrapped up the last lesson."

Zach scratched his jaw. "Yeah, you mind if Joanna grabs some food with us? I kind of dumped it on her that she's on her own this trip, and I think she's a little upset about it."

A woman stepped up to Zach's side with her hands

wrapped around a coffee cup. "Hey, I'm Joanna. We've met a few times before."

"Oh, yeah!" It was all coming back now. Joanna was Zach's younger sister. "We met at college." Aiden remembered seeing her at least once at the dorms where he and Zach had lived at the University of Colorado.

She hadn't changed enough to be unrecognizable, but she had acquired an air of sophistication and maturity that intrigued him. Her blonde hair rested lightly on her shoulders, and her light-brown eyes were friendly and matched her smile.

He extended a hand to her, and she accepted it. Her touch was warm from the coffee she held, and he held on a few seconds longer as his fingers thawed.

"Zach didn't tell me you were coming. Welcome to Freedom Ridge." Aiden lifted his arms at his sides to encompass the enormity of the high country.

"He didn't tell me you worked here either," Joanna pointed out as she narrowed her eyes at her brother.

It was interesting watching the siblings interact. He liked that she didn't let her brother get away with anything. Zach was Aiden's best friend, but he'd be the first to admit that his buddy needed a swift kick in the pants every once in a while.

Zach huffed a sigh. "I didn't think it mattered. But, hey, we're all here now!"

Aiden crossed his arms over his chest and widened his stance. "So, do you snowboard too?"

Joanna laughed. "Oh no. I wouldn't know what to do in the snow. I'm used to the warmer weather in Phoenix."

Aiden stepped forward to allow a man to pass behind

him. Fortunately, the move brought him closer to Joanna. He could smell her perfume. Definitely vanilla. "Does that mean you'll be taking some lessons? I think I can squeeze in a few next week."

"No you don't. Joanna isn't the snowboarding type," Zach interjected.

She furrowed her brow and squared her shoulders. "Says who? I could learn."

Aiden tried to hide his grin as Joanna held her ground. He respected anyone who stood up and spoke for themselves, but he was fascinated by her reaction. There wasn't an ounce of doubt in her posture as she lifted her chin.

"Yeah, but you've never done anything like that before," Zach reminded her.

Joanna's gaze didn't waver from her brother. "That doesn't mean I'm incapable. You'll be on the mountain with Aiden the whole time we're here. What else am I supposed to do?"

Aiden watched in awe at Joanna's determination. It was the kind of passion he liked to see in his students, and it was nice to know she was up for trying something new. Why wouldn't Zach encourage her?

"Actually, I don't get as much time to play as I'd like," Aiden corrected. "I teach lessons two days a week, and I work two days on and four days off at the fire station."

"So you have some days off?" Zach asked.

"Yeah, but depending on my shift at the station, that next day might consist of mostly sleeping," Aiden said. "If we run a lot of calls, forty-eight hours feels like a hundred."

"That's a bummer." Zach turned to his sister. "Looks like you've got more time with me than you thought."

Aiden loved the hustle of the Christmas season, but he found himself wishing for a slowdown this year.

"I'm starving," Zach huffed.

"Let me get changed, and I'll meet you at the restaurant," Aiden said.

"Sounds like a plan. Joanna and I will grab a table."

Aiden headed toward the staff lockers where he kept his extra clothes, but he stole a glance at Joanna over his shoulder. She was feisty and gorgeous, and he was having a hard time looking away from her.

He scrambled through his thoughts for anything he could remember about her, but nothing stuck out to him. She'd been young when he was in college, but whatever age difference existed between them didn't seem so gaping now. He quickly changed his clothes and brushed his hair before heading to the restaurant.

The Liberty Grille had a variety of foods and a view to write home about. Snowy mountains covered the area as far as the eye could see, and Aiden never tired of the breathtaking view.

His attention was normally drawn to the scenery first, but Joanna stood in the outdoor seating area on the other side of the expanse of windows. She was facing away from him with a camera raised to her face.

He watched her for a moment, studying her controlled movements as she captured photos of the place he loved.

A cough drew his attention to the dining room. Zach was waving Aiden over to a table with a scowl on his face.

Great. Zach had probably caught him staring at Joanna.

"What were you doing?" Zach asked as they took their seats at the table.

Aiden rested back in his chair. He didn't need to look at the menu. "Just enjoying the view."

Zach narrowed his eyes. "The one you see every day?"

"It never gets old."

"Come on. You were looking at Joanna. I'm not stupid." Zach's tone held a hard edge that grated on Aiden's nerves.

"What if I was looking at her? She's pretty."

Pretty wasn't the word he wanted to use, but it would suit the conversation with her brother. Gorgeous or stunningly beautiful were more accurate descriptions, though her features weren't generically pretty. She possessed a unique look like no one he'd seen before, and he was fascinated by the subtle aesthetics of her features.

Zach leaned his elbows on the table and leveled Aiden with a serious look. "She's my little sister. Keep your distance."

Aiden sat forward. "You're kidding. I haven't even said anything, and you're calling her off-limits?"

"That's exactly what I'm doing. Here she comes."

Zach sat back in his chair as if nothing had happened. Aiden, however, still wanted to throat chop his friend.

Joanna pointed to the windows. "That view is going to be so hard to leave. I can't believe you live here, Aiden." She took a seat beside Zach and adjusted the napkin in her lap.

She looked like a kid in a candy store with her face lit

up in excitement. Aiden wanted to capture that happiness and carry it around with him every day.

"I can't believe it either sometimes," Aiden said. "You should see it from the slopes." He might have been taunting his friend with that last comment, but Zach deserved it if he was going to be a jerk to his sister.

Joanna picked up the menu. "Maybe I will get to see it."

Aiden scooted forward in his seat. "So, you're up for snowboarding?"

"I don't know about all that, but I'd like to get outside for some photos."

Zach rested his menu on the table. "Joanna is a paralegal, but she used to do photography and graphic design in high school and college. She took a bunch of classes."

"That sounds interesting," Aiden said.

"It has its days, but it's nothing like photography." She shrugged. "Photography is just a hobby, though." She brushed her hair over her shoulder. "I'm sure it doesn't hold a candle to snowboarding for a living. And did you say you were a firefighter too?"

Aiden smirked at his friend. Flames practically burst from Zach's glare. "Yeah, I love my jobs."

It was nice catching up with his friend during their meal, but Aiden found himself sneaking in any comment or question to find out more about Joanna. He told himself that including her in the conversation was polite. If Zach hadn't been so weird about Aiden admiring Joanna earlier, he would be outright flirting right now.

After dinner, Joanna stood and waved. "Well, gentlemen, I think I'm going to call it a night."

"It's barely nine," Aiden said.

Joanna covered a yawn. "Traveling has zapped my energy."

"Right. What about tomorrow?" Aiden asked.

"I don't know. What are the plans, Zach?"

Zach shrugged. "I was thinking we could hit the slopes."

"Go have fun." She waved them off. "I think I'd like to spend the morning taking some photos of the decorations. I haven't seen a place this decked out for Christmas in years."

Aiden waved back as she moved away from their table. "Suit yourself. See you later."

"Night, sis."

"Good night," she called back to her brother.

Before Joanna was out of sight, Zach growled, "Could you stop hitting on my sister?"

Shocked by the seriousness in his friend's tone, Aiden crossed his arms over his chest. "I'm not hitting on her. We need to include her or else she'll be bored by herself within the week."

Zach sighed and rubbed his hands over his face. "You're right. Sorry. Maybe I need to turn in early too. I've been up since dawn."

Aiden clapped a hand on his friend's shoulder and stood. "Get some shut-eye. You're going to need it if we're boarding tomorrow."

"I know. It takes me a few days to get back in the groove of things." Zach stretched and stood. "I'll catch you in the morning."

"See you," Aiden said, waving two fingers in the air at

his friend. He still had a twenty-minute drive home, and daylight would come before he knew it.

The drive home was quiet and sheltered by the pines leaving too much space for Aiden's thoughts to wander to Zach's warnings about Joanna.

Aiden didn't even know her. He shouldn't be looking for ways around his friend's big brother protectiveness anyway. She would only be in town for a month, and Aiden would be staying. His life was here, and hers was back in Phoenix.

He'd feel better about the strain between Zach and himself after they spent a day on the mountain. As much as he wanted to see Joanna again, he needed to back off a little... for now.

## 3

_J_oanna turned in every direction, unsure where to focus her attention. Every inch of the lodge was elaborately decorated. Inside, outside, and from top to bottom—lights, garland, and ornaments adorned the tourist hub. She spent the morning photographing the trimmings in the lounge, as well as the stunning view. If a picture was worth a thousand words, she could write an epic love story with the gallery she'd captured in the two days since she arrived at Freedom Ridge.

Joanna adjusted the settings on her camera and took a test photo of the garnished hearth. The resort should make the elaborate decor a focal point of their marketing for the holiday season if they hadn't already.

"The hearth is probably my favorite of all the decorations," a nearby woman said.

Joanna nodded. "It's a stunning display."

"It's nice to know you think so." The woman's red hair hung over one shoulder, and her eyes were full of friendliness. "It takes weeks of prep to manage this." She gestured to the lounge with pride.

"The view is certainly worth the effort. I could spend hours photographing just this room."

The woman extended her hand. "I'm Haven. I'm the event planner here. You should check out the outdoor decorations next. I love planning outdoor weddings during the Christmas holiday."

Joanna shook hands with the friendly woman. "Thanks for the tip. I'll definitely check it out and hopefully get some amazing photos."

"I'm sure you will. Enjoy your stay."

Haven waved her good-bye, and Joanna went back to capturing the glints and lights of the decorations. Checking her watch, she realized it was close to lunchtime, but the Mountain Mug coffee bar smelled enticing. She stepped into line and ordered a chai latte. Propped against the corner of the bar, she planned her next round of photos while waiting for her drink.

"Looks like a lot of work," a male voice said.

The voice sounded familiar and grated on her nerves. She finished making the appropriate adjustments to the settings on her camera before she responded. "I'm sure. The event planner just told me it takes them—"

Her words clogged her throat as she found herself face to face with Keith Sanders.

"What are you doing here?" she asked sternly. Of all the people she might run into on vacation, Keith was the last person she wanted to see.

Keith smiled and linked his hands behind his back. "I'm on vacation."

The barista called Joanna's name, and she accepted the drink with a shaking hand. Why was he so calm and collected as if it wasn't a crazy coincidence that they'd ended up at the same place hundreds of miles from where they lived? It didn't take much for her thoughts to negate the crazy coincidence option.

"No, *I* am on vacation. What are you doing in Freedom?" There was no excuse for his presence here in the remote place she'd chosen to spend Christmas with her brother. There was also no patience in her tone.

He was close enough that his shoulder almost brushed hers, and her skin prickled at the proximity. She stepped away from him and straightened her posture. Following her to a different state was unacceptable.

"I'm enjoying myself. It's... interesting here."

He wasn't even pretending Freedom Ridge was a potential holiday destination in his mind. He almost sneered when he said the word *interesting*.

"Keith, did you seriously follow me here? How did you know I was coming to Freedom?"

Keith held up his hands in surrender. "I'll admit, when I saw you, I thought it was a welcome coincidence as well. How convenient that we ended up at the same place to spend our vacation."

"No, it isn't convenient. Who told you?" Joanna demanded. She was losing her patience with his innocent act.

"Relax. I'd love to get to know you while we're both here. It's such a romantic place." He extended his arms to indicate the decor.

Keith was definitely following her. There wasn't any

way they ended up at the same place otherwise. She'd underestimated his infatuation, and now she'd have to find a way to avoid him all while keeping an eye on him.

"How long are you staying?" she asked.

"Through the new year."

She'd been working around the clock for months to make sure she could take a month off from work. How had Keith been able to reschedule his calendar for a month to take the same time off? He laid out of work frequently. She felt her neck beginning to burn with her anger.

"I have to go." Joanna turned on her heel and sped from the lounge as fast as her booties could carry her.

Keith's elevated protests followed her up the stairs, but she wasn't about to give him a chance to follow her. She needed to get out of his sight.

In the safety of her room, she pressed one palm against the door and focused on the cool surface beneath one hand and the hot chai latte in the other to calm her racing heart. She'd wanted the latte, but she wasn't sure she could stomach it just now.

Perhaps she was overreacting. Keith hadn't tried to harm her. He hadn't even asked her on an official date this time. Granted, she hadn't given him much of a chance.

Joanna pulled her hand from the door and shook it. No, she was sure he'd followed her here. Who would do something like that? A stalker? Was it even considered stalking if he only followed her *once*?

But if that one place was to another state where she'd be spending the next month, his actions held much more weight.

She needed to call Chris in the human resources department at Miller and Baker. Sitting on the bed, she removed her phone from the camera bag and made the call. She tried to calm her nerves while the phone rang, but each breath shook as she exhaled.

"Miller and Baker. This is Chris."

"Hey, it's Joanna Drake." She'd spoken to Chris before when they'd crossed paths, but this was her first complaint.

"Hi, Ms. Drake. What can I do for you?"

"I wanted to talk to you about Keith Sanders. I'm on vacation for the next month in Freedom, Colorado, and Keith just showed up here claiming he's vacationing here as well. What are the odds of that?"

Chris pondered the question with a hum. "It's possible. Has he harassed you in any way?" His tone wasn't condescending, only matter-of-fact.

"Not really, but he's been asking if he can take me to dinner for weeks now, and I've told him numerous times that I'm not interested." When she said the words out loud, it sounded like harassment.

"I see your concern," Chris said. "I'm checking his file, and it looks like he put in a notice for the time off back in July. It seems his vacation was planned well in advance."

"In July?" Joanna questioned. "When exactly in July?"

"July 10."

"Is there any chance he could have overheard me talking about my vacation plans at the Independence Day picnic?" She'd booked her own trip at the end of June and had been giddy about it at the picnic.

"Perhaps. Has he threatened you in any way?"

"No. I just wanted to let someone know. For the record." Doubt was creeping into her tone, and her phone call suddenly seemed rash.

"I've made a note of our conversation, and we'll look into his actions. Please let us know if something happens."

Of course, it would be too late if she was supposed to let him know *after* something happened. Dread settled over her like a cold sheet. "Thank you, Chris."

Joanna cradled the phone in her hands after ending the call. Was she overreacting?

Needing to validate her instincts, she called her friend Brandi.

"Hey, what's up?"

Brandi had been her neighbor and friend for years. She was a social butterfly, always encouraging Joanna to step out of her comfort zone and try something new.

Joanna picked at the plastic lid on her coffee cup. "Not much. Just sitting in the room."

"Why are you in the room?" Brandi asked. "You're on vacation."

"I was downstairs in the lounge, but Keith showed up, and…"

"Wait," Brandi interrupted. "Creepy Keith from work?"

Joanna sighed. "Yes, that one."

"He's *there*? Why? How? That's nuts!" Brandi's rapid-fire questions confirmed her outrage.

"See? I knew it was weird for him to show up here on *my* vacation. The HR department at Miller and Baker pretty much brushed it off." Joanna's anger was back, doubled at being dismissed for her concerns.

"Do they know he's a persistent weirdo?" Brandi asked.

"I told them he'd been asking me out."

The rumble of a car passing muffled Brandi's end of the call. "Did you tell them you told him no in fifteen different languages?"

Joanna stood and paced. "I did, but Chris in HR pointed out that Keith hasn't harassed me or threatened me. Can I really make a complaint about him for being annoying?"

"No, but you can put your foot down when he follows you to Colorado," Brandi pointed out.

"Yeah, Chris said Keith put in a request for this time off months ago. It's legit as far as they're concerned."

"That's stupid." Banging sounded on Brandi's end of the call. "Sorry. Dropped my phone." She sounded out of breath. She liked to multitask and often ended up fumbling everything.

"Agreed. Now I'm hiding out in the room until Zach and Aiden get back from snowboarding."

Brandi's voice rose in pitch. "Aiden? Who is Aiden? I know you're not talking about Zach's super cute room-mate from college."

"Oh, but I am. He works here, and Zach failed to tell me until yesterday."

"You lucky dog. Is he single?"

Joanna huffed. "I don't know, but it doesn't matter. He lives in a different state, and I'm only here for a month."

"So?" Brandi questioned. "You need to loosen up and have a little fun, Jo."

"You have enough fun for the both of us." Joanna tried

to conceal the hurt in her tone. It wasn't Brandi's fault if their friend roles were based on their personalities. Brandi was the easy-going fun one, and Joanna was the stern responsible friend.

Brandi's voice held a hint of pity. "I know you're waiting for the right man, and I don't ever want you to settle, Jo. God knows the man He has for you, and you'll cross paths with him when it's time. But for the next month, you can have fun with Zach's cute friend. I wish you could forget about work and your extreme sense of responsibility to a company that doesn't care about your wellbeing and be free."

"You're right." Joanna had checked her emails not two minutes after opening her eyes this morning. "I need to make the most of the vacation and take advantage of the opportunity."

"That's my girl. Now, I need your help deciding which Christmas parties to attend. There are too many, and I can't be in multiple places at once." Brandi was a master at networking and made a friend of everyone she met.

"I'm the last person you should be asking. I'm not attending a single party this year."

"That means you're better at saying no than I am. I want to go to *all* of them, but I can't decide which I'll have to miss."

"Don't think of it as missing a party. You'll have a great time wherever you decide to go."

Brandi giggled. "Are you saying I'm the life of the party?"

"You are. Now, let me hear the list."

Joanna helped her friend sort through her social

calendar while she drank her chai latte. She had a month left at Freedom Ridge, and she didn't want to spend it hiding from Keith. If only she had someone with her to serve as a buffer for Keith's advances.

She was tired of worrying about it for now, and decided she'd wait for Zach and Aiden to return before going back downstairs.

**4**

---

$\mathcal{H}$aving Zach back on the slopes was a nice break from the all-work-and-no-play cycle Aiden had been repeating for months. December was one of the busiest times at the resort, and knowing he'd have a friend to break up the long work days was already boosting his morale.

"Dude, how do you do this every day? I'm so out of shape." Zach massaged his quad muscles.

"You get used to it." Aiden clapped his friend on the back. "You need to get out of the office every once in a while."

"Yeah, but the coffee shop doesn't run itself." Zach grumbled something about joining a gym.

As much as Aiden had enjoyed the day on the slopes with his friend, he was eager to get back to the lodge and hopefully see Joanna again. He scratched at an itch on his wrist just below the cuff of his winter gear. "What's Joanna doing tonight?"

Zach cut Aiden a grim look. "I'm not sure. She probably took pictures all day."

"It's kind of sad that she's all by herself," Aiden pointed out. They were getting close to the lodge, and he resisted the urge to pick up the pace.

"Yeah, but she'll be doing some work too. She's a workaholic."

"So, it runs in the family?" Aiden asked.

Zach shoved his friend's shoulder. "I can't slack, man. The coffee shop is a lot of work."

Hustle and Brew had been Zach's dream since they started college together. Owning the coffee shop had always been his goal as they worked their way through their business classes.

Aiden had followed a different dream. Business hadn't been his true calling, and he'd gotten smart about it right after college. Being trapped in an office for eight hours a day would be torture.

Grasping for a light approach to the subject that he couldn't ignore, Aiden kicked his boot in the fluffy snow alongside the trampled path leading to the lodge. "We should invite Joanna to the Christmas parade."

Zach scrunched his nose. "Christmas parade sounds lame."

"Everyone goes. Christmas is a big deal in Freedom, and I think Joanna would like it. Did you see the way she was looking at the decorations last night?" Aiden certainly hadn't missed her fascination.

"Seriously, get Joanna out of your head. She's not your type anyway."

Aiden wasn't sure he had a type. His dating history was sparse and fleeting. "Why not?"

Zach pulled his beanie off and rumpled his hair. "She's just not. I know she's a grown woman, but she's still my little sister, and I don't want her to get hurt."

Aiden jerked as if he'd been electrocuted. "I would never hurt her."

"Not like that." Zach waved him off. "I mean, she doesn't date a lot, and as assertive as she is in her business life, she isn't as confident when it comes to dating."

"Why not? She's beautiful, intelligent, nice…"

"Will you *please* back off?" Zach's tone held a sharp edge. "You're not the kind of man she needs."

"What's that supposed to mean?" All rational thought flew out the window as Aiden questioned his friend. Was he looking for a fight? Maybe. But he wasn't about to lie down and let Zach tell him he wasn't good enough.

Zach gestured to the mountains around them with wide eyes. "You live here. You do what you love, and you don't have to answer to anyone. Joanna is responsible and loyal. She's generous and thoughtful to a fault, and she needs someone who knows how to be part of a whole."

Aiden didn't speak. Zach's description of Joanna made her sound even more appealing, widening the gulf between them.

"She just needs commitment because, when she finds the one, she'll be all in. I'm not sure you're an *all-in* kind of guy."

Aiden let his friend's words sink in as they arrived at the lodge. He'd given his friend reason to believe he couldn't be loyal to a woman, and the truth hurt. He wanted to be that man, but it meant he'd have to make it known in his actions.

Just because he didn't have someone in his life didn't mean he wasn't capable of being selfless in a relationship. He hadn't found the woman he wanted to spend his life with yet, and he wasn't about to rush it.

Still, this month with Joanna could be a chance to get to know her.

A month. He only had a month with her, and a busy month at that. Maybe Zach was right. How could it work out between them in the long run if she didn't even live here?

The thought left Aiden feeling hollow, but his friend was right. Things between him and Joanna had little chance of working out. It'd be best to focus on spending time with Zach on the slopes.

Zach pointed toward the stairs leading to the guest rooms. "I'm gonna change. I'll meet you back down here in fifteen and we can grab a bite."

"Sounds good." Aiden made his way to the staff lockers and cleaned up. Fifteen minutes later, he stepped into line at Mountain Mugs for something to warm his insides.

"There you are." Joanna appeared next to him. "Zach didn't answer my text."

Aiden's blood pumped with adrenaline in his veins at the sight of Joanna. What was it about her that piqued his interest in a way that no one else did? "He just went up to his room to change. What's up?"

She wrung her hands and scanned the room. "Nothing. I was just wondering if I could hang out with you and Zach tonight. Unless you had something planned."

As if the opportunity to spend time with her had fallen into his hands, he grabbed it and held on. "Nah, we were just about to get something to eat. You're welcome to join."

Her shoulders relaxed, and her smile appeared. "Thanks. I've been kind of bored all day."

Aiden stepped out of the line for coffee. He didn't need the pick-me-up anymore. "There's a lot to do here. I can talk to Haven about the activities and get some brochures for you."

"The event planner?" Joanna asked with a tilt of her head. "I met her today. I liked her."

Knowing she was at least making friends eased some of Aiden's concerns about her sitting alone at the lodge all day.

"I'll definitely ask her about some things to do around here the next time I see her." Joanna's gaze bounced around the room before landing on her watch. "How long did Zach say he'd be?"

Aiden looked around too. "He should be here by now. I'll call him." The call rang five times before picking up Zach's voicemail.

"Maybe he fell asleep," Aiden said with a shrug. "We had a big day today."

Joanna shook her head, but a slight smile lifted the corners of her mouth. "That sounds like something Zach would do."

"Why don't we at least get a table? They fill up fast around here." Aiden's hand instinctively went to the small of her back as they walked, and he pulled it away quickly. With Zach breathing down his neck, he'd have to think about his actions. Their earlier conversation seemed ridiculous after the ease he felt after spending a few minutes with Joanna.

"Oh, we can order if he isn't here soon. Zach won't care."

They were seated at a table, and Joanna seemed to settle. Her gaze still frequently scanned the room, but her shoulders relaxed as the waiter came to take their orders.

It would be easy to spend a quiet evening alone with Joanna, and Aiden found himself leaning in as she spoke.

"So, how did you end up in the legal field?" He might only have a few minutes alone with her, and he wanted to take advantage. She had his undivided attention.

"My dad was a lawyer, and he said I had a knack for it. I enjoy the paralegal side much more than the actual attorney work though. He taught me the ropes when I started working at his firm in college, and I never considered doing anything else. I work for a different firm now, but I love what I do."

Aiden knew the ease of doing what he loved for a living, and he was glad Joanna had that excitement too. It made getting up for work each morning less of a chore. "Zach may have mentioned that you were a workaholic." Aiden lifted one brow in question.

Joanna chuckled. "He's one to talk."

Her gaze no longer bounced around the room, but it focused steadily on Aiden. The pull toward her intensified, and he forced himself to stay in the conversation. "I know. I tell him he should move out here and work at the resort with me."

"Oh, Zach wouldn't leave the coffee shop." Joanna

waved a dismissive hand. "So, did you and Zach talk about me?"

Caught between a rock and a hard place, Aiden cleared his throat. "Your name may have come up."

Joanna grinned, but her cheeks flooded with color. "I'm afraid to ask what you talked about."

Remembering the conversation, Aiden's expression fell. "You don't want to know."

An uncomfortable silence joined them at the table until their food arrived. By the end of the meal, their conversation had drifted to lighter topics as she questioned him about living in a tourist town, but Zach still hadn't shown up.

Joanna looked at her watch. "Should we check on Zach?"

"He's probably fine, but you can knock on his door if you want."

She wrung her hands for a moment as she eyed the stairs.

Aiden gestured to the majestic mountains outside the windows of the restaurant. "Snowboarding can be exhausting. He was complaining about the workout earlier."

Joanna nodded, agreeing with him. "You're probably right. I bet he fell asleep."

Aiden leaned closer to her and asked, "Would you like to hang out with me tonight? It's cold out, but there are some fire pits outside where we could talk."

A slow smile lifted her lips. "I'd like that."

Aiden stood and extended his elbow to her. "Let's check in on Zach first." She rested her hand in the crook of his arm and tucked in close. Zach could step around the corner at any moment, but Aiden couldn't take his eyes off Joanna. The two sides of his brain were at war, and the one that relished the company on his arm was winning.

He should be happy to be standing next to Joanna Drake. Not only was she beautiful, but their conversation over dinner had been lively and fun. He'd have to find a way to spend time with her without having to look over his shoulder all month.

"I'll just run up and check on him. I'll be right back."

He watched Joanna bounce up the stairs, hoping he'd be able to spend the evening with her alone.

## 5

When Joanna knocked on Zach's door, he'd answered sleepy-eyed to tell her he was napping and would call her later. She sped back down the stairs to meet Aiden and found him waiting in line at Mountain Mug. With warm drinks in hand, they found a fire pit and moved their chairs close enough to feel the heat on their faces and the cold night on their backs.

Joanna settled into her chair and blew the top of her hot coffee. She wasn't worried about Keith here—not with Aiden so close. Even without her brother around this evening, she hadn't felt the need to watch out for her crazy coworker.

The fire crackled, and she rubbed a hand over her blistering face. "How did you end up in Freedom?"

"I've always lived here. I went away to college for a few years—that's where I met Zach—but I grew up in Freedom."

She tried to imagine what it might be like to live here. At least in the month of December, it was bustling with tourists wrapped in coats and happy families enjoying the Christmas festivities. "I bet it was fun growing up in a tourist town."

Aiden leaned back in his chair and stretched his legs out in front of him. "Yes and no. Everything changes, and you have to learn to go with the flow. A lot of my friends left after high school."

Joanna hadn't kept up with many of her high school friends either. They'd scattered to the winds chasing careers. "I feel like Phoenix never changes. Or if it does, I never notice." The latter might be closer to the truth. She often found herself so absorbed in her work that she failed to see life passing around her. Time seemed to pass slower in Freedom, and she noticed more in each moment.

"What made you decide to come to Freedom this year?" he asked.

She took a soothing sip of her coffee and breathed in the cold air through her nose. The hot and cold mixture cleared her mind. "Mom and Dad wanted to spend the holiday with our brother and his new family. He's been married for a couple of years now, but this is their son's first Christmas. David and his wife live in Houston, so Zach and I just told our parents to go and enjoy baby Lance's first Christmas. I wouldn't want them to miss that."

The fire cast dancing shadows on Aiden's face. "I bet they're thrilled about the grandbaby."

"Oh, you have no idea. David is the oldest, but our parents have been dropping hints that they want grand-kids for years. My brothers and I have all been victims of our parents' blunt reminders that they aren't getting any younger."

Aiden laughed. "My mom does that sometimes too, but she's a little more subtle about it. I know she doesn't want to pressure me, but she'd be an awesome grandma." He stared at the fire as the smile faded from his face. "She gets lonely."

"Does she live around here?" Joanna asked.

"She was born here, and she'll die here if she has any say about it. She manages the bakery in town, Stories and Scones. It keeps her busy, and she loves it."

Joanna smiled as she imagined Aiden's mother bustling around a bakery and greeting locals and tourists alike. What did she even look like? Would she have Aiden's dark hair and expressive eyes? "What about your dad?"

Aiden stared at the fire and took a deep breath. "My dad died a few years ago. He had a heart attack."

A pang of hurt filled her chest for Aiden and his family. "I'm so sorry."

Aiden hung his head. "Yeah, he was the best. I'm a lot like him. He was always up for something new and exciting. He wasn't afraid of anything." He ran his thumb along the rim of his cup and grew silent.

"I can't imagine what that must be like. I still have my parents." She couldn't stomach the thought of losing them. She'd been blessed with a wonderful family that loved immensely and looked after each other no matter what. It was inconceivable that one of them could be gone.

Aiden nodded. "It's been hard, especially for my mom.

She's always been a happy, upbeat person, and I know it's taking everything she has to keep going. But she never lets her resolve slip. She might not be smiling every day, but she only cried around me a couple of times. She was trying to be strong for me while I was trying to be strong for her."

Joanna swallowed hard and looked into her coffee cup. "You're lucky to still have each other."

Aiden grinned, and the firelight lit up his green eyes. It was as if a flame danced within them. "We are. I try to spend some time with her at least once a week. She has friends at the bakery and church, but I want her to know I'm still here too."

Joanna scooted closer to him. "Speaking of church, where do you go around here? I'm going to be here for a month, and I'd like to find a local place."

Aiden scratched the back of his neck, looking uncomfortable. "I used to go to Freedom Bible Church, but I haven't been in a while."

"Why not?" Joanna asked. "If you don't mind telling me, that is."

Aiden lifted one shoulder noncommittally. "I was raised in church, and I believe in God. I just… kind of drifted away after Dad died."

Every fiber of her being told her to reach out to him. She wasn't sure what the nudge meant, but she decided to take a leap of faith.

Resting her hand on his arm, she gained his attention. "I can't imagine what you went through when you lost your dad, but God didn't do this to punish you."

"I know that. I just haven't felt close to God in a while.

It's my own fault, and I'm ashamed I've let myself drift so far away. My mom is disappointed in me too."

"Hey," Joanna whispered, giving his arm a gentle squeeze.

Aiden lifted his gaze to meet hers, and with them both propping their elbows on their knees, they were mere inches apart.

"It's never too late to be forgiven."

Her words hung in the air around them, and his gaze didn't waver from her. She swallowed hard as nervousness crept up her spine. He was so close, and he was looking at her as if he wanted to say something important.

His lips parted, but another voice broke the silence.

"What are you doing?"

Joanna jumped back in her seat and turned toward Zach. "We... I thought you were sleeping."

Zach crossed his arms over his chest, and the light from the fire illuminated his scowl. "I was."

"We figured as much," Aiden said. "You put in a good run today."

"Yeah," Zach grumbled.

Shaken by Zach's sudden appearance, Joanna stood and stretched. "I think I need to turn in for the night. It was nice talking to you, Aiden."

"I had a great time too. Good night."

Joanna breathed a shy "Good night" before stepping past her brother without a word. His grumpy attitude didn't sit well with her, and she didn't want to stick around for more.

"I'll walk you to your room," Zach said as he fell into place beside her.

"Suit yourself, but I know the way."

Zach sighed as they stepped into the lounge. "It's not that. I wanted to talk to you."

"Are you ready to tell me what has your face all scrunched up like a pug?" she asked.

"Come on, Jo. You don't need to get involved with Aiden."

"Why exactly would you care?" She wasn't involved with Aiden. It wasn't as if they were having some scandalous affair or something. They'd had dinner and talked. There wasn't any harm in it, and she'd had a nice night.

She set her course for the stairs leading to her room. Talking with Aiden had been more than nice. She remembered the way he'd leaned in when she spoke, and a flush crept up her neck.

Zach scrambled to keep up with her brisk pace. "He's just not the right guy for you."

Joanna turned on her heel and squared her shoulders to her brother. "How would you know? You know nothing about the men I date, and you're not my dad. Stop acting like you can tell me what to do."

Of course her brother wouldn't know about the men she dated. That was because she rarely dated at all. There weren't many men that she felt a connection to, and being with Aiden felt right. She couldn't explain it, but she knew in her heart that she needed to get to know him better.

Zach's brows scrunched together. "Quit playing."

"I assure you, I'm not playing."

"You know what I mean."

She resumed her speedy walk down the hall toward her room. "Please tell me how Aiden is good enough to be your best friend, but he's not good enough to spend an evening talking to your sister."

Zach ran a nervous hand through his hair. "It's just a guy thing. You wouldn't understand."

She reached her door and dug into her pocket for the key card. "Thankfully. That would be awkward."

"Just… don't get too attached, okay?"

Joanna opened the door and stepped inside. "Good night, Zach."

She let the door close between them and hunched her shoulders. Her brother had an uncanny way of erasing the good from an amazing night.

She took her time changing into pajamas and washing her face before she slid under the covers of the strange bed. It had been years since she'd taken a vacation, and she wasn't used to sleeping in a bed that wasn't hers.

With the lights off and the room quiet, Joanna prayed.

"Dear Lord, my heart is heavy for Aiden and his family. I know it's been years since his dad passed, but I hope they've found peace." She opened her eyes and stared at the white ceiling. "Please help me find a way to show Aiden how to open his heart to You again."

She closed her eyes and felt a warmth in her heart. It was as if she were being told to stay close to Aiden. "How?" she asked. Did he need her ministry? Could she help him see how much he needed God in his life?

"Help me to see Your path for me, Lord. Amen."

She rolled over and realized she didn't get Aiden's phone number. If she wanted to see him again without her brother hanging over her with a frown, she needed to find a way to get in touch with him.

With a relaxing breath, she decided to wake up early and see if she could catch him in the lounge before Zach woke up.

She didn't like sneaking around her brother, but nothing that Zach warned her about made sense. Trusting her heart, she made a plan to meet Aiden.

**6**

---

$\mathcal{A}$iden sipped his coffee in the lounge. He liked to be early, and Zach wasn't supposed to meet him for another twenty minutes. That meant he had plenty of time to enjoy his coffee and say his good mornings to the guests who milled around getting ready for their daily excursions.

His boss, Kevin, spotted him across the lounge and made his way over, greeting him with a hearty handshake.

"Hey, you remember Nathan Douglass from a few weeks ago?" Kevin was the kind of manager everyone dreamed of having. He remembered everything, which worked in your favor if he caught you doing something good. He also made a point to make friends with the people he worked with. He and Aiden had hit it off from day one.

Aiden wasn't the best at remembering names, but Nathan had made quite an impression with his larger-than-life personality during their lessons. "Sure. Why?"

"His dad left a beaming review on Google where he

went on and on about how his son had the best time taking snowboarding lessons from Aiden. You were the star of the review." Kevin clapped a hand on Aiden's shoulder.

Aiden sipped his coffee. "That's awesome. He was fun to work with. Maybe they'll come back for another visit."

Kevin adjusted his glasses, still grinning from the news. He took pride in managing a welcoming resort. "The review said they were working on scheduling another vacation to Freedom Ridge Resort already. Keep up the good work."

"Any time, boss." The two men slapped hands as Aiden spotted Joanna descending the stairs across the room. "Catch you later."

He couldn't take his eyes from her as he dodged guests to get to her. She'd seen him too, and it seemed she was on a path to meet him. Although he might have been wishing her eagerness into existence.

"What a beautiful way to start the morning," he said when they met.

Her smile widened, and she touched her earlobe as if searching for an earring. "Good morning to you too. I was hoping I'd catch you before Zach made it out of bed."

Intrigued, Aiden stepped closer and scanned the stairs for any sign of her brother. "Really? What can I do for you?"

She grabbed his hand, and every nerve in his palm fired off tiny explosions to his fingertips. He squeezed her hand in his, unwilling to let her go quickly. She tugged him toward a corner where they would be out of plain sight and turned to face him. He kept his grip firm as his heart rate accelerated at their proximity.

Joanna made sure they had a clear view of the stairs and whispered, "I didn't get your number last night."

His morning was getting better by the minute. "I didn't get yours either. We were interrupted." Their whispered words made their talk by the fire the night before sound a lot more scandalous than it was. It had been quite the opposite—relaxed and casual.

"Speaking of that interruption, Zach seems to think we shouldn't be hanging out. I know he has good intentions, but it's annoying when he tries to tell me what to do."

Ice formed in Aiden's veins at Joanna's revelation. "He said the same thing to me."

Joanna picked at her fingernail and dropped her chin. "Maybe he's right. I mean, I'm only here for a few more weeks."

His gut was twisting tighter with every word she said. "I know, but I had fun talking to you the other night. I don't think it would hurt to just hang out."

As soon as he said the words, he knew they were lies. If he grew attached to Joanna, it *would* hurt when she had to leave. Why was he advocating for more than they had? Wouldn't it be the smart thing to do to let sleeping dogs lie?

"I guess so. I know I want to hang out with you, but maybe we should just stick to friends."

"You haven't even known me for four days and I've already been friend-zoned," Aiden jested.

Joanna chuckled. "Don't be sad. You won't have to

worry about splitting your time between me and my brother this month."

Aiden's smile fell as he realized he was disappointed that he wouldn't even get a chance to see where things could go between them. "Zach will be down soon. Let me give you my number." He held out a hand for her phone and typed it in.

She recited hers next, and they returned their phones to their pockets.

"What are your plans for today?" he asked.

"I thought I would look for something to do in town."

Aiden made sure Zach wasn't coming and said, "You want to meet up in town tonight?"

Her eyes were glowing with mischief. "I thought we were supposed to stick to friends."

"I can meet up with a friend for dinner. Especially if that friend is you." He couldn't break his gaze from hers. It was as if his mind was on autopilot.

"How are you going to get past my stick-in-the-mud brother?" she asked, leaning in closer to whisper.

Aiden couldn't breathe. She was too close, and he was too tempted to either say things that would lead to deeper feelings or lean in and seal his lips with hers. "I'm sure he'll be tired of me after I leave him in the dust on the slopes today."

She looked around again. "We've got our work cut out for us."

"Is that a yes?" he asked, hanging on her answer.

She bit the side of her bottom lip as she contemplated her answer, and he couldn't look away. "I guess so. How's your stealth?" she asked playfully.

"I've got stealth in spades. Don't worry about me."

"Arrogant."

"I like to think of it as confidence." He certainly felt confident right now. Joanna had moved so close that it would take two inches of movement to kiss her.

Joanna cut a glance to the stairs and stepped back. "Here he comes."

"Meet me at Giovanni's at seven. It's on main."

"Got it. See you then." Her smile was bright and infectious.

There was a heartbeat of indecision where he felt an undeniable urge to kiss her in the stolen moment they had, but the chance had passed when she stepped out of the alcove and blended into the guests filling the lounge.

Aiden watched her move through the room for a moment, unable to look away. He hadn't expected Joanna, certainly not like this. She stirred a new life inside of him that he wanted to awaken more every day.

How had he failed to notice her in college? Maybe that hadn't been their time. She'd still been in high school, and she hadn't lived in Colorado.

She still didn't live in Colorado, and that was one fact he needed to keep reminding himself about. Maybe it would dampen the feelings that were growing all too fast for a woman he'd just met.

Zach talked about his sister like she didn't know how to have fun, but Aiden had seen her playful side this morning when she'd been the one to instigate a private rendezvous.

Aiden saw Zach scanning the room and stepped out to meet his friend. Normally, he would be excited to spend a day snowboarding for fun instead of teaching lessons, but today, he found himself wishing he were exploring his tiny hometown of Freedom with a special someone.

"Hey, you ready?" Zach asked as he spotted Aiden.

"Sure. Let's go."

Aiden brushed a hand over the scruff on his jaw as he took one last look at the lounge on his way out. He spotted Joanna on the other side of the room, and she was watching him with a smile.

He definitely wanted to stay here with Joanna today, but he needed to find a way to make her brother okay with them hanging out first. If he brought up the subject too often, Zach would get all big brother protective again.

Aiden's mind warred with the options. It seemed there were more reasons pushing against them, but that one reason to go for it was much stronger than the others.

## 7

*A*iden had said she would love the little town of Freedom, and he was right. Main Street was bustling with lights and bells, and a dusting of snow completed the Christmas scene. Quaint shops lined the streets, and many artists created their unique crafts in the front windows of the stores for everyone to see.

Joanna had spent the afternoon picking up extra gifts for her family and friends from the local shops. She checked her watch before making her way back to Zach's car. Her arms were full, and she needed to Google the address for the restaurant Aiden had mentioned.

Settled in the warm car, she studied the map on her phone. Giovanni's was only two blocks away. She craned her neck to check the street name at the intersection behind her and stopped short. Keith was walking down the sidewalk on the opposite side of the street.

She ducked her head back and stayed still, praying he didn't spot her. Zach's windows were slightly tinted, but she could only hope Keith would be distracted by the Christmas decorations.

He looked around as if he were searching for something, but his gaze didn't fall on her. When he was out of sight, she breathed a sigh of relief. Why did he evoke such strong reactions from her? It was almost instinctual. Though he hadn't made known any intentions to harm her, he had no regard for her wishes when he ignored her each time she declined his dinner offer.

Freedom was a small town, and she had to believe it was only coincidence that she kept running into her coworker. If she kept her eyes open and alert, maybe she could stay one step ahead of him.

Joanna yelped and clutched the front of her coat when someone knocked on the car window. After a couple of deep breaths, the tingling in her skin subsided and she pressed the button to roll down the window. "Aiden, you scared me."

His grin was friendly but slightly ashamed. "I'm sorry. I didn't mean to sneak up on you. I just spotted you from across the street and thought we could walk to Giovanni's together."

Joanna nodded. "Of course." She grabbed her purse and joined Aiden in the street. Stepping onto the sidewalk, she had the urge to reach for Aiden's hand. The instinct was irrational, but it seemed the natural thing to do while walking down the street of a Christmas town with a handsome man.

She wrapped her arms around her middle, pulling her coat tight around her.

"Are you okay?" Aiden asked. "You seem a little skittish."

Joanna brushed her hair from her face. "I'm fine. Just trying to get over the scare you gave me when you knocked on my window."

Aiden chuckled. "You act like I caught you with your hand in the cookie jar." He wrapped a strong arm around her shoulders and pulled her in close to his side. "I didn't mean to scare you. Can you forgive me?"

Joanna smiled and leaned in to his warmth. She felt a tug in her middle and wondered if it was the sensation people often described as butterflies. "I'll consider it. You'll have to bribe me with food first."

Aiden held the door open for her as they stepped into Giovanni's. "I'd be happy to."

Pushing thoughts of Keith from her mind, she focused her attention on Aiden during dinner. He was kind, fun, and easy to be with, and she had to remind herself often that she was leaving soon. Her vacation would come to an end, and Aiden would stay here in Freedom when it came time for her to return to her life in Phoenix.

She found herself flipping back and forth from enjoying Aiden's company to replaying her brother's warning in her mind. Zach was right when he said it couldn't work between her and Aiden. Their lives weren't in sync.

*This is not a date. This is not a date with a handsome man that you just happen to love hanging out with.*

Aiden entertained her with stories about his firefighter friends as they ate, which saved her from talking too much about herself. If he asked point blank about her skittish mood again, she might just tell him everything about Keith. It was becoming difficult to dodge her coworker without having someone to talk to about it.

"So, my buddy, Carson, he's a no-nonsense kinda guy, and we decided it was his turn to get pranked. He never wanted to be in on the fun, but we couldn't just leave him out. We took it easy on him and filled his locker with down feathers."

Joanna let out an uninhibited laugh before clapping her hand over her mouth to stifle the noise.

"When he opened the door, they went everywhere. Carson grumbled about the mess for a week before he got us back."

Joanna leaned on her elbows over the table. "What did he do?"

Aiden leaned back in his chair and grinned. "He hid all of our toothbrushes."

"Where?"

"Everywhere. We each had a scavenger hunt." Aiden chuckled at the memory. "It took Quintin two hours to find his."

Joanna wiped her eyes and breathed through belly laughs. She hadn't been this relaxed in years. Her lighthearted mood might be attributed to the winter air, but she was pretty sure it had more to do with her carefree date.

But it wasn't a date. She and Aiden were only friends. Maybe she just needed more nights like this with friends.

To make that happen, she'd have to find more friends. The only person she hung out with back home besides her family was Brandi.

She checked her watch and gasped. "It's nearly nine. I bet Zach has called me a dozen times." Sure enough, her phone was flooded with missed calls and texts from her brother.

"I need to call him." She stuck the phone to her ear, and Aiden didn't protest.

"Hey," she said as soon as Zach answered. "Sorry I missed your calls. I've been in town, and I forgot to check my phone."

Zach sighed. "I was worried, Jo. I assumed you'd be back by now, and I had no idea where to start looking for you in town. I don't know my way around."

Joanna looked across the table at Aiden, who was waiting patiently to hear how the call was going. "I know. I'm so sorry. I'm on my way back now."

"Great. Knock on my door when you get in. I want to know you made it back safely."

"Sure. See you in a few." Joanna hung up the call and faced Aiden. "I have to go. Zach is worried. I can't believe I lost track of time." It wasn't so inconceivable. She'd been having fun.

"I haven't been checking the time either. Will you call me when you get in and let me know you made it?"

His concern for her safety reflected her brother's. She smiled knowing she was well protected if she had Aiden and Zach looking after her. She didn't need to worry about Keith.

"I will. Thank you for dinner. I had a great time."

"Let me walk you to your car."

Once again, she found herself itching to reach for Aiden's hand as they walked along Main Street. Snow was beginning to fall like tiny feathers, and the twinkling Christmas lights gave the entire town the illusion of a holiday movie.

When they reached Zach's car, Aiden opened the driver's side door for her and waited next to the car while she buckled her seat belt. "I know it's just a dusting, but I think I might need to follow you back to the lodge."

Joanna turned up the heat and rubbed her hands together. "You don't have to do that. I promise to call when I get there. I have your number now." She winked. Winked! It was brazen and fun flirting with Aiden.

"Okay, but you have fifteen minutes." His warning sounded more like a challenge.

She started the car. "I'd better get going then."

"Please be careful." Now he sounded genuinely concerned, and those butterflies were back in full force.

"Of course." She shifted the car into gear and made an effort to drive as cautiously as possible. She'd never driven in snow before, but the roads were fairly clear. Aiden had told her they treated the roads regularly due to the harsh weather.

With both hands on the wheel and both eyes on the road ahead, she made it back to the resort and parked in the parking garage within ten minutes. She had plenty of time to knock on Zach's door and call Aiden before he sent out search and rescue.

Joanna tugged at her scarf as she entered the lounge and immediately spotted Keith sitting casually on an oversized sofa near the fireplace. She stumbled into a clumsy twirl as she switched direction and took the path to the stairs that was farthest from Keith. She shoved her back against the nearest wall as if she were the star in a made-for-TV spy movie. Peeking around the corner, she waited until he was distracted by a middle-aged woman before darting around the corner and up the stairs.

She gave Zach's door three solid knocks on her way down the hall and checked over her shoulder as she inserted the key into her door. No one had followed her.

With the door firmly closed behind her, she leaned against it and prayed. "God, why am I afraid of him? I've never felt like this before." Ever since he'd followed her to Colorado, she'd been thinking of him as stalker Keith instead of creepy Keith, and it made all the difference.

"Dear Lord, what do I do?" she whispered into the quiet room.

Maybe she just needed to breathe. Keith hadn't approached her again, and maybe he didn't intend to. Perhaps she'd jumped to a very big conclusion when she'd labeled him a stalker.

Remembering her promise to call Aiden, she pressed the button to dial his number as she settled onto the bed.

"Just in time."

"Don't call for a search party yet. I made it," she joked.

"Thanks for calling. I'm not used to worrying so much over someone, and I'm..." Aiden stumbled over his words and sighed. "I'm just glad to know you're in safe for the night."

She felt the relief in his words. It was just the two of them on the line, and he'd all but confessed to caring about her on a level that surpassed casual friendship.

"I had a great time tonight," she whispered.

"I did too. I won't see you for a few days, but you could text me if you want. I might even get to call a few times."

Joanna fell back onto the bed and closed her eyes as the soft comforter cradled her. He was calling and texting like a boyfriend, but they weren't supposed to be together. They'd agreed on friends. Still, she couldn't force herself to push him away. "I'd like that. I'll be with Zach most of the time, but I'll answer if I can."

"Good night, Joanna." The deep timbre of his voice soothed the tension from her shoulders.

"Good night, Aiden."

She disconnected the call and lay still and quiet on the bed. She'd be with her brother for the next two days while Aiden worked his shift at the fire station, but after that, she needed to come up with a way to stick close to one of them.

She contemplated a way to get Zach to agree to let her hang out with him and Aiden, but sleep found her before she'd found any answers.

## 8

"*A*iden!"

Aiden jumped at Carson's shout just behind his chair. "Good grief, did you have to yell?"

"Well, I didn't the first and second time, and you didn't hear me. Are you off in la-la land?"

"Maybe." He'd been relaxing in the common room at the fire station, engrossed in a text conversation with Joanna. "What's up?"

Carson jerked a thumb over his shoulder to the kitchen area of the fire station. "We're ordering pizza. You in?"

"Sounds good. The usual."

Carson placed the order and settled into the recliner nearest Aiden. "I'm spent, and we still have twelve hours to go."

"I heard that," Aiden agreed. "I need about two days to catch up on sleep."

His phone dinged, and he quickly reached for it.

Joanna: How do you put up with Zach for long periods of

time? He's driving me crazy.

Aiden smiled and began typing a response, but another text came through.

Joanna: He said I could go snowboarding with the two of you on Friday, and he's being picky about the clothes I need to buy.

Heart racing, he typed faster, but she beat him again.

Joanna: I'm not really snowboarding. I just want to take some pictures from the slopes.

Aiden had erased and retyped his message three times. He was excited to see her again, even if they wouldn't be together a lot of the time.

His face fell when the problem surfaced in his thoughts. How would he hide his growing attraction to Joanna from Zach?

"What's with the long face? You look like you swallowed a bug," Carson said.

Aiden sighed. "There's this woman."

"Shocker. Is there ever another reason men get a long face?"

"Only when a dog dies," Aiden said.

Both men shuddered at the thought.

"If you're making that sour face when she texts, why are you responding?"

Aiden shook his head. "It's not her. It's her brother."

"Oh." Carson threw his hands in the air. "I don't want any part of that debacle."

"It gets worse," Aiden said. "He's my good friend."

Carson whistled. "Are you sure she's worth it?"

Aiden propped his elbows on his knees and rested his head in his hands. "The answer is yes and no. Yes because

I like her. She's great. But it's no because she doesn't live here. She's a guest at Freedom Ridge Resort."

"No way. Nuh-uh. Back off now. Don't get attached when she'll be leaving. That will never end well."

"Thanks," Aiden bristled. "Tell me how you really feel."

"I'm just saying. You're in for a world of hurt, and so is she."

Aiden scrubbed his fingernails through his hair. Not only did he have her brother to worry about, but he seemed to be conveniently forgetting she was leaving. "I don't know what to do."

"I just told you. Put it in reverse and back away from that dumpster fire. It won't end well."

But Joanna was anything but a disaster. Zach had said she was a workaholic, but she hadn't picked up her phone once throughout their dinner together. She wasn't the stick-in-the-mud her brother made her out to be. She was going to the slopes with them later this week, and that was a welcome start. Maybe he could even get her on a snowboard before the end of the month.

"What I'm hearing is that you don't have any advice for me about how to handle her brother."

"None." Carson stood and stretched. "I have to get up and move around or I'll fall asleep before the pizza gets here."

Aiden picked up his phone and read her texts again. Indecision clouded his heart, and he remembered Joanna's words from the night they'd talked by the fire pit. An urge he hadn't felt in years grew within him.

He needed to pray.

He hadn't prayed since he'd watched his dad's casket

sink into a hole in the ground, but he remembered how to do it. His dad had been the one to teach him to pray at an early age, and he'd be ashamed to know it had been so long since Aiden had spoken to the Lord.

Closing his eyes, Aiden prayed.

*Lord, I'm sorry. I've been living a life for myself. I don't know how to fix what I've done—or not done—these past few years, but I know I'm ready to try. I'm asking forgiveness, for stepping away from You for so long.*

His apprehensions lifted as he prayed, and he continued.

*I feel like You sent Joanna to me. She isn't the only one who has told me I need to get right with You, but... maybe she just said the exact words I needed to hear. She's been good for me, Father, and it may be selfish of me, but I really want to get to know her more. I know You may have another plan for us, but she's been great. I just don't know how it can work.*

Aiden lifted his head and sighed. *Let me know what to do, please. I want to do what's right. What You would have me to do. Amen.*

He opened his eyes and looked around the room. Nothing had changed, but he felt different. It was as if he'd taken a step in the right direction. His phone sat beside him with an unread text from Joanna. He hadn't even heard the ding of the alert.

Joanna: You're probably on a call right now, so I'm praying you stay safe.

Aiden started at the words. They'd been praying at the same time, and maybe that was the only thing they could do—the best thing they could do.

Pray and trust that God had a plan.

## 9

*J*oanna spotted Aiden in the lounge before he saw her. Hanging back, she didn't approach him. They had a long day ahead of them, and she didn't want to start it off with Zach's grumpy warnings if he caught her flirting with his friend. It had been four days since she'd seen him and a week since they'd met, but those butterflies were here to stay.

She made her way to Mountain Mug and found her place at the end of the long line. Keeping her eyes open for Zach, she snuck glances at Aiden as he spoke to a man with dark hair and glasses across the room.

The lounge was full of people, and she found it difficult to watch the entire room. Her neck twisted one way, then the other, looking for Zach, then Keith, then Aiden over and over again. The influx of sights and sounds was giving her a headache. She really needed that coffee.

She'd just gotten her drink from the barista when she spotted Zach beside Aiden. Taking her time, she added sugar and creamer to her drink before joining the two men by the door.

"Good morning. You ready to get a real view of the Rockies?" Aiden asked with a smile.

"Good morning to you too. I can't wait. If it's anything like the view from the restaurant, you might have to drag me in kicking and screaming this evening."

Zach grinned and leaned on his board. "You'll love it. Are we ready to head out?"

"Let's go," Aiden said, holding the door for Joanna and Zach to step through.

Joanna adjusted the settings on her camera as they moved outside. The sun was blinding as it reflected off the crisp white snow. "So I'll just ride with you to the top and take the gondola back down later."

"Sure," Zach said. "We'll meet you in the lobby around five for dinner."

She wouldn't actually get to spend much time with Zach and Aiden today, but that was okay. There would be plenty of people around, and that was enough to settle her anxiety.

The men walked a few steps ahead of her, and she lifted her head to watch where she was walking. "Aiden, where is the best—"

Her sentence was cut off by Zach's yelp as he stumbled on the first step of the stairs leading down to the lift. Joanna and Aiden both reached for him, but his body twisted as he tried to catch himself on the handrail.

Zach fell down the five stairs in hard bumps and thuds that seemed to shake the ground beneath her before he landed in a crumpled heap at the bottom.

"Zach!" Joanna cried.

She and Aiden rushed down the stairs. Zach was groaning and slowly pushing himself up when they descended on him.

"Stop. Don't move," Aiden demanded. "Just stop for a second and tell me if anything hurts."

"Good grief." Zach rubbed the back of his head. "I hit my head, but it doesn't feel like a concussion."

Her brother had played football in high school, and she remembered at least two trips to the emergency room when he'd been too confused to know his own name. "Are you sure?" she asked.

"Yeah. It's just a bump." He shifted his weight and sucked in a hissing breath through his teeth. "And my ankle." Throwing his head back, he sighed. "You've got to be kidding me. I'm here to snowboard!"

"Not anymore," Aiden confirmed as he straightened out Zach's leg. "Let's get you up." Aiden braced an arm under Zach's shoulder, and Joanna scrambled to lift his other side.

Aiden and Joanna helped Zach hobble back to the lounge where they settled him on one of the oversized couches and propped his foot on an ottoman.

"What now?" Zach asked with a huff.

Joanna braced her hands on her hips. "I think you need to get to a doctor and see what kind of damage you have."

Aiden jerked a thumb at her. "What she said."

"I am not about to spend my vacation at a doctor's office. This is ridiculous."

"What's ridiculous is messing up your ankle because you didn't take good advice. You could do some serious damage. It's best to just get the recoup started." Aiden folded his arms across his chest in a serious stance.

"I'll go with you," Joanna offered.

Aiden stood, ready to help. "Me too."

"I'll bring the car around." Joanna held out her hands to Zach for the keys.

He rolled his eyes and threw his head back against the couch. "Fine."

She accepted the keys and made off for the parking garage. She pressed the button for the elevator and checked that her camera was secure in its case while she waited.

"Hey, I was starting to think this was a bigger place than I expected," Keith said beside her.

Joanna didn't turn to him as she finished zipping the camera bag. She couldn't even offer a response as she silently worked to control her breathing. The last thing she wanted was for him to know exactly how much he got under her skin.

The elevator doors opened, and Keith gestured for her to enter first. The skin on the back of her neck prickled as she stepped in front of him. She didn't like it when he was behind her. She didn't like it when he was anywhere near her, but what choice did she have?

Pressing the button for the underground garage, she stepped back and waited to see where he would go. When he didn't press a button for another floor, she discreetly pulled her phone from her pocket and pressed a few buttons until she could call Aiden with one touch. Being alone in a parking garage with stalker Keith sounded like a scene in a horror movie.

"Where are you headed today?" she asked as casually as possible. If she knew where he was, she wouldn't have to keep such a keen eye out for him.

"I was actually looking for you. What are you doing?"

That was the answer she'd feared. "I'm just grabbing my brother's car. He hurt his ankle, and I need to drive him to the doctor."

"That doesn't sound good. Maybe I'll catch you later. Would you like to meet me for dinner?"

The elevator doors opened, and she stepped out backwards, keeping her body facing him. "I think my brother needs me. I don't want to leave him alone."

Keith's expression gave nothing away. "I see. Maybe tomorrow."

"I have to go." She turned her back to him when their conversation was over, but he stepped out of the elevator behind her. Forcing herself not to turn around, she prayed he wasn't following her. She had to turn a few corners to get to the row where Zach's car was parked. She was relieved to see that Keith hadn't followed her when she reached the vehicle. The less he knew about her, the better, and she definitely didn't want him knowing which car she would be driving

She took a few slow breaths through her mouth as she started the engine, glad to be driving away from the resort for the rest of the morning.

## 10

*A*iden sat in the waiting room while Zach saw the local family doctor. Joanna had paced the room no less than a dozen times and flipped through every magazine on the table.

Certain that Zach's injury wasn't more than a sprain or a strain, he reached for Joanna's hand as she paced by him. "Hey."

She turned to him as her hand rested in his. His skin hummed where they touched, and he found himself at a loss for words as her brown eyes stared into his.

Aiden cleared his throat. "He's going to be fine. It's probably not anything major."

She nodded and looked at the door leading to the exam rooms. "I know."

Was she trying to convince herself that her brother would be fine, or was she restless because of something else? "Do you want to take a walk in the parking lot? I'll go with you."

She nodded again. "Sure. I think I need to get out of here."

They stepped outside, and she wrapped her scarf around her neck. Her somber expression didn't change with the new atmosphere. "Every time I walk outside, it's like someone is waking me up with a bucket of ice on my head," she jested.

"It takes a long time to get used to cold like this. It's extreme, but it has its perks."

"Like what?" she asked.

"Like idyllic Christmas settings, winter sports, and picturesque mountains. Speaking of, I'm sorry you didn't get to take any pictures today."

Joanna waved a dismissive hand. "It's no big deal. I'm here for a few more weeks. We can try again when Zach is feeling better."

In a brave moment, Aiden suggested, "Or you could come with me one day."

Joanna cut a glance at him and smiled. "I could."

"You could also go to dinner with me, if you wanted to."

She tilted her head and sighed as they walked along the perimeter of the parking lot. "I *want* to, but…"

"There's the but."

She chuckled. "But there are a few reasons we decided it was best if we stayed friends."

"Like your brother's fierce protectiveness and the fact that you live hundreds of miles away?" Aiden tried to keep his tone light as he recounted the facts he'd been chewing on for a week.

"Yeah. Those reasons." She dragged the toe of her boot

through the soft snow. "Why does Zach think we shouldn't see each other?"

"Because your brother was around for my college years."

"Oh," she drawled. "Were you a partier or something?"

"No, not that. I guess he has the impression that I'm selfish because I haven't ever had to think of someone else first. I'm an only child, and while I don't consider myself spoiled, I just didn't have anyone to answer to. I respect my parents, and they raised me well, but I went and did what I wanted, as long as I wasn't hurting anyone or being stupid. I wasn't reckless or thoughtless, so my parents never put a lot of rules on me. I was a pretty good kid."

She shrugged. "Then what's the problem?"

"Zach thinks you need a selfless man. Maybe someone with commitment experience. I don't have that." He rubbed a hand over his face. "To some extent, I agree with your brother. I want to live up to the man you deserve, but maybe I'm not there yet. I told you I haven't been close to the Lord in a while, and you made me realize that's something I need to change."

"That's a good thing. I don't expect you to be perfect. I know I'm not. I fail and fall short all the time." She stopped walking and rested a hand on his arm. "But I could tell when we talked that you were feeling some regret for losing touch with God, and to me that says you might be ready to make things right."

Aiden covered her hand with his. "I am. Thank you for setting me straight, but it reminded me that I have a long way to go."

She smiled. "We're all a work in progress. That won't ever stop."

Her understanding was a greater mercy than he'd ever experienced from another person, and he fought the urge to kiss her. Joanna was special, and he would be a fool to let her get away.

"I'd like to have dinner with you. Tomorrow night. As friends." The last words cut through his joy like a sword, but he would rather have dinner with her as friends than miss spending time with her.

She studied him as if contemplating her options. "Okay."

Aiden released a breath that clouded in the cold air.

She looked to the doctor's office across the parking lot. "We'd better go see if Zach is finished."

"Right. Maybe we should have dinner somewhere besides the resort tomorrow night," Aiden suggested.

"That's probably a good idea. What's your favorite place?"

"There's a local restaurant you might like on Main. I'll pick you up at the resort at six if that's okay."

"It sounds good to me. Zach is pretty tired of me after we spent two days together."

Aiden chuckled. "I'd trade places with him in a heartbeat."

She shoved his shoulder playfully. "Hanging out with me is different from hanging out with you on the slopes. He was definitely bored."

They stepped inside the doctor's office to find Zach at the checkout window. He wore a boot on his right leg and leaned against crutches.

"How'd it go?" Aiden asked.

"Slight fracture. I need to come back next week for a follow-up, and I have this extra equipment at least that long."

Aiden held the door for them to exit. "What about recovery time?"

"At least a few weeks. I'm non-weight bearing this week."

"That's not terrible," Joanna said. "Especially since you have me to help."

Zach lifted one corner of his mouth in a grin. "Thanks, Jo. I'm sorry you've had to spend so much of this trip by yourself."

She shrugged. "It's been nice. I've had a great time so far."

He adjusted his crutches and moved closer to hug her. "You're the best."

Aiden cleared his throat. "I'll bring the car around."

Zach handed him the keys and started making his way down the steps on his crutches.

Joanna had agreed to dinner with him, but why did he feel guilty for keeping it from his friend? He wasn't dating her—she'd made that clear. Still, Aiden felt a gnawing uncertainty as he started the car. He wanted to spend time with Joanna, but it came at the cost of keeping things from his friend. After seeing their sibling bond, he knew he didn't want to do anything to jeopardize the relationship they had.

He'd have to work harder to make sure he wasn't anything more than friends with Joanna Drake.

## 11

*J*oanna pulled her scarf up around the sides of her face as she waited for Aiden at the front entrance of the lodge. The last thing she wanted was to be spotted by Keith, and she was preoccupied watching for Aiden to arrive.

Zach had piddled around the lounge most of the day before resigning himself to his room for the evening to watch a football game. It was a good thing because she was tired of holding her tongue every time her brother moaned and groaned about his terrible lot in life. She was one complaint away from kicking his crutch out from under him.

She felt bad for him, but he wasn't accepting his fate with grace at all. He was too busy lamenting the loss of snowboarding hours to see that there were other fun things to do in Freedom.

Aiden's truck pulled into the portico, and Joanna darted out to meet him before he could make his way around to open the door for her.

"Hey," he said with a smile as she settled into the truck. "You ready to go?"

"So ready." She rubbed her hands together and blew warm air into her palms. "It's freezing out here."

"It only gets colder as the winter moves on. Are you wearing layers?" he asked as he shifted into gear.

"All the layers. Who knew those wool-lined leggings my mom gave me for my birthday would come in handy?"

"When is your birthday?"

"January nineteenth. What about you?"

"July nineteenth. We're exactly six months apart."

Joanna shook her head. "Couldn't be any more different."

"I wouldn't say that," Aiden said. "I think we're a lot alike."

"Oh, yes," Joanna jested. "I'm a fun-loving outdoor adventurist with two physically demanding jobs, and I live in a super cute tourist town in the frigid mountains."

Aiden chuckled at her description of him. "You *are* fun, and you *are* up for a little bit of adventure. We're both close with our families, and we both put up with your brother."

Joanna nodded. "You're right. We're both patient and selfless for not thumping him in the head every day."

Aiden cut his glance at her as he drove. "We both love the Lord."

Joanna grinned and whispered, "That too."

"So,"–Aiden slapped his hand on the wheel— "are you ready for the best chocolate mousse cake you've ever tasted?"

"Yum. I couldn't say no to that."

Aiden parked on the street next to a blush-colored Victorian house with white trim and a sign out front that read Evelyn's.

"This is it?" Joanna asked. "It's beautiful."

"I thought you'd like it." Aiden jumped out of the truck and ran around the front to open her door.

Inside, the smell of meat and spices greeted her as she removed her scarf and coat. "It smells delicious."

"Wait until you taste it," Aiden said.

The dark wooden walls and gold trimmings gave the place a warm feeling of comfort, and the Christmas decorations were over the top. The hostess led them to a table in front of a large window that looked out over the mountains.

"What a view." Joanna settled into her seat. "I could sit here all day."

Aiden chuckled as he lifted the menu. "I would eat myself sick if I sat here all day. The food is so good."

When their waiter arrived, Aiden ordered the garlic roasted lamb, and Joanna chose the brown sugar glazed salmon.

Joanna couldn't keep her gaze from roaming the room. At first, she was only admiring the beautiful decorations, but looking around reminded her of how she'd spent her entire vacation scanning rooms for any sign of Keith.

"Joanna?"

She jerked her attention to Aiden. "Yes."

"Is everything all right? You seem distracted or… nervous."

She sighed and weighed her options. If she told him

about Keith, she wouldn't have to watch out for him alone anymore.

"I haven't said anything to Zach yet, but I think one of my coworkers followed me here."

Aiden's brow furrowed. "What do you mean? Are you saying he's stalking you?"

Joanna shrugged. "I don't know. Back at home he's been asking me to go to dinner with him for weeks, and I've told him no every time without hesitating. Then, he shows up here as soon as I arrive, and apparently he's staying the entire time I'll be here."

"That's insane. Why haven't you said anything?"

"I did. I actually reported it to the human resources department at my company the day I found out." Joanna shrugged. "They weren't very concerned because he hasn't threatened or harassed me." The memory of the dismissive phone conversation grated on her nerves.

"I'd say he's harassing you if he won't take no for an answer. And that's not okay. No one should mess with you like that or have you looking over your shoulder constantly. That's not okay," he repeated.

"What am I supposed to do about it? I've just been avoiding him any chance I get."

"Let me set him straight," Aiden said with a frown. Determination settled on his face.

She reached across the table and laid a calming hand on his. "Listen, I don't want trouble. If he does something, then we'll talk. I don't want to make a big deal if he really is harmless, but I also don't want to dismiss him since he *could have* followed me on vacation. I'm just being overly cautious and... aware."

Aiden scrubbed a hand over his face. "I think you need to stay close to either me or Zach. I don't like this at all."

"Trust me, I don't like it either. Why do you think I've been trying to tag along as much as possible?" she asked.

Aiden feigned shock. "I thought it was because you couldn't resist me."

Joanna laughed, but the joyful sound was short-lived. "I don't understand why Zach thinks it wouldn't work between us. I mean, I know I don't live here, but I think we make a good team." She shrugged. "And it's just hanging out, right?"

Aiden leaned forward and fixed his gaze on her eyes, then her lips, before lifting back to her eyes. "Is it?"

Her body flushed with heat as the breath she'd been taking died in her lungs. Aiden had a way of stopping her in her tracks with his intensity. "Isn't it?"

He didn't look away, but she had to break the connection. He was seeing too much, and she was feeling things a little too deeply for "just hanging out."

She leaned back and cut the tether that had held them steady. Moving her gaze around the room, she focused in on a familiar form. "Oh no. He's here."

"Who?" Aiden immediately turned to see who she'd referred to.

"Don't look. It's Keith."

Aiden's attention snapped back to her like a magnet. "The coworker?"

"Yes. He's here." She shielded her face with her hand. "There's no way he could've known I was coming here. Freedom is a little too small sometimes."

Aiden craned his neck to look for Keith again. "Which one is he?"

"Please don't look," she begged. "I don't want to draw attention.

Aiden turned back to her with a grimace. "Too late. Looks like he's coming over."

## 12

*J*oanna's shoulders tucked in as Keith approached their table. This was a side of her Aiden hadn't seen before, and he hated it. She shouldn't cower to anyone.

"Hey, Joanna. It's good to see you here." Keith was probably just under six feet with a lean build and a penetrating voice that was too high.

"Aiden, this is Keith." She stressed that last word to pronounce it clearly.

"Ah," Keith drew out in a nasally tone. "You must be Joanna's brother."

Fire pumped through Aiden's veins as he watched Joanna stumble over the introduction. In a split second decision, he stood and offered his hand to Keith. Aiden made sure to catch the man's attention. "I'm Aiden, Joanna's boyfriend."

Keith's hand hung limp as Aiden applied a little too much force in the handshake.

Joanna stood, but Aiden held Keith's stare, daring the man to look away.

"Joanna told me about you. Funny thing you decided to vacation at the same place where we'll be celebrating our first Christmas together."

Keith's pallor grew bleak, and his jaw bobbed a few times before he stammered, "Uh, yes, it is a coincidence."

Aiden released Keith's hand and wrapped his arm around Joanna's shoulders. "We've been trying to spend as much time together as possible. You see, I work at the resort, so I'm always around." Was he laying it on too thick? It didn't matter. He wanted to give the guy as many warnings as possible.

Keith's color was returning, and his shock was morphing into apparent irritation. He pursed his lips, and his gaze darted back and forth between Joanna and Aiden. "I didn't know Joanna was seeing anyone. Funny she hasn't mentioned you."

"I'm a private person," Aiden explained.

Keith chewed on the inside of his cheek for a moment. "It was nice seeing you, Joanna." He turned and walked off without looking back.

When he was out of sight, Joanna settled back into her chair with a sigh of relief. "I think that may have solved the problem. I can't believe you said you were my boyfriend." Her cheeks were pink, and she covered them with her hands.

Aiden forced his breaths to come more evenly to calm his anger. "I can't believe he's following you around. And the boyfriend thing just kind of came out. I'm sorry I didn't run that by you first."

"Are you kidding? It was genius. Thank you for being so… bold."

The appreciation in her words and her eyes was cooling the heat of his anger. "It wasn't such a stretch. We're having dinner together."

"That we are," Joanna agreed. She bit the side of her bottom lip and sighed. "Thanks for doing that. I feel so much better."

"You think it put him off?" Aiden asked.

Joanna shrugged. "I'm not sure, but I think he'll at least be a little more reserved around me from now on."

"I have to work the next few days at the station, but if he approaches you again, just tell Zach or call me. I'll tell my boss about this, and there's a security guard at the resort I'll introduce you to." He'd call Kevin and Heath tonight and fill them in on Joanna's situation along with a description of Keith.

"I haven't told Zach about him yet, but I'll stick close to him while you're gone. That has kind of been my plan this whole time."

Aiden shook his head. "I don't like that guy."

Joanna picked at her fingernails. "I don't either. I was direct and clear when he first started asking me out. Then, I kind of got a little stern. Now, everything has changed since he showed up here. I feel like I should be cautious around him."

"You should. You never know with people like that. His mood changed too quickly in the few seconds he spoke to us."

"You're right. I'll just hang around Zach."

"Are we going to continue being a couple around

Keith?" Not that Aiden ever wanted to see Joanna's coworker again, but being Joanna's boyfriend sounded like a good idea.

Joanna shrugged. "That's up to you, I guess."

"I think we should. He needs to know you're being protected. I know I can do that without pretending to be your boyfriend, but he'll think he can't get a date with you as long as you're in a relationship, so why ask?"

"What about Zach?"

"Stick with him when I'm not around."

"No, I mean, should we tell Zach about the fake dating?"

Aiden pondered her question. "That's up to you. I know we're not really dating, and that's what he's against, but how will we explain how this all started?" They couldn't tell him they'd run into Keith while having dinner together.

Joanna huffed. "If only he wasn't so dead-set against us hanging out, this would all be much easier."

"Yeah, but he just cares about you. And maybe there isn't any reason to get him in a huff if we aren't really dating."

"True. But what if we're all together and Keith shows up? We'd have to play the part, and Zach wouldn't be in on it."

"That might blow our cover," Aiden admitted.

"I'll tell him," she said.

As much as he wanted to *really* be dating Joanna, he wouldn't care if she shouted it from the rooftops. "Okay."

Their food arrived, and they talked about the menu,

the town, and the photos she'd taken since she'd arrived in Freedom. The rest of the night was the perfect date. Aiden's attention often drifted to her mouth when she told him about photographing the sunset in Australia when she was in college. He couldn't take his eyes off the curves of her neck when she would pull her hair around to fall over one shoulder.

After dinner, they stepped out into the bitter cold, and she tugged her coat tightly around her middle. "Would you mind if we walked down Main a little way? I saw a chocolate shop the other day, and I'd like to get Zach a truffle."

"Sure. I could use a treat myself."

Aiden tucked his hands into the pockets of his coat as they walked side by side. His instinct was to reach for her hand, but he knew the only relationship he was destined to have with Joanna was the fake one he'd thrown them into an hour ago.

Entering the warmth of Freedom Fudge Factory, Joanna found a mint chocolate truffle for Zach. Aiden requested two chocolate-covered strawberries and prayed she would like it.

The bell above the door chimed as they stepped back out onto the sidewalk of Main Street. Christmas lights, garland, and trees filled almost every inch of the town square.

"What did you get?" she asked.

Aiden narrowed his eyes at her. "Do you like choco-late-covered strawberries?"

"Who doesn't?"

He pulled one of the fat strawberries out of the bag and handed it to her in the thin paper cup. "One for you." He pulled the other out for himself and crumbled the bag in his hand. "And one for me."

Joanna laughed. "We already had dessert at Evelyn's." They'd shared a chocolate mousse cake that she'd said was the best she'd ever tasted.

"Second dessert is a thing."

Joanna touched her strawberry to his and said, "Cheers," before shoving the pointed end of the strawberry into her mouth.

"Wow," Aiden remarked. "It's either been way too long since I've had one of these or this is amazing."

Joanna made an affirmative humming noise in her throat. "It's so good."

They'd finished their treats by the time they had walked back to his truck, and he opened the passenger door for her. Once she was in her seat, he inched closer and didn't close the door.

"I don't think I'll get to take my time and say a proper good-bye when we get back to the lodge—in case Zach is hanging out in the lounge—but I want you to know I had a great time with you tonight."

Joanna twisted her hands in her lap and smiled. "I had a great time too."

Aiden knew there were reasons they couldn't be together, but right now, he couldn't recall a single reason why he shouldn't kiss her good night. He wanted to lean in, seal his lips with hers, and then whisper promises that every night could be this way.

Then a cold shock of reality slid down his back. He couldn't do any of those things.

Instead, he stepped back, closed the door, and drove her back to the lodge. At the lodge, he whispered a heavy good-bye as she leapt, grinning, from his truck.

## 13

*J*oanna accepted two cups of coffee from the barista at Mountain Mugs and made her way over to the couch where Zach waited. The resort had a gym, and they'd spent the morning there when he'd gone stir crazy after breakfast.

The improvised workout had settled him enough to get through lunch without fidgeting, but at four in the afternoon, his uninjured leg was beginning to bounce again. She hadn't anticipated the effort it would take to convince an active, grown man to elevate his swollen ankle.

"Here you go. Black and boring." She handed him the cup of caffeine knowing it was a bad idea.

"Just like my heart."

"Oh, come on," Joanna admonished. "You've just been... a little cranky lately."

"You noticed?" Zach removed the lid from his cup and let the steaming liquid breathe. "It's Stacy."

"Stacy Callahan? Your old girlfriend from high

school?" Joanna hadn't heard that name in years, but Stacy had once been like a part of the family. She had always been around.

"The one and only." Zach threaded his fingers through his hair. "She came to Phoenix to visit her parents a few weeks ago, and we met up."

"And?" Joanna sat forward in her chair, eager for more of the story.

"And I miss her. A lot."

"Where is she living now?"

Zach flopped back on the couch. "Wyoming."

"Wow. That's a long way from Phoenix. What's she doing up there?"

Zach waved his hand in the air. "She's a veterinarian. She loves horses, so she does house calls for the ranches and rodeos."

"Sounds like a dream job."

"Yeah." Zach closed his eyes and blew out a breath. "I have the coffee shop. It's doing great. I can't leave it, but I... want to." His sentence trailed off as the truth was given voice.

"You want to move to Wyoming for her?" Joanna asked in a high-pitched voice.

"I don't know!" he growled. "I know I want to be with her, and moving doesn't seem like that big of a deal if I could be with Stacy."

"But you haven't been together in what, eight years?" Joanna asked.

"Ten," Zach corrected.

She whistled. "That's steep."

"But we're still the same people. If we hadn't gone to different colleges, we would be married by now."

"Married! You've never mentioned marriage before." Who was this stranger and what had he done with her brother?

Zach made a tsk noise out of the side of his mouth. "That's because Stacy hasn't been around the last ten years."

The hurt in her brother's voice had her chest aching. She wanted him to be happy, but was it right for her to encourage him to go after something so far-fetched? Was it right for her to wish for something equally as far-fetched? Hadn't she been trying to find a way to make a long-distance relationship seem manageable? If she and Aiden didn't live so far from each other, she was certain they'd make a great team.

"Listen," Joanna rested her hand on Zach's shoulder. "I want you to be happy, and I remember Stacy. She was kind, and she loved you. I can't imagine she's changed much. If she's the one, maybe you need to think about how you can make it work."

Zach threw his forearm over his eyes. "Forget it, Jo. It's stupid."

"It's stupid that you'll purposely not go after something that makes you happy simply because it's a *person* and not a *career*?"

He sat up and gave her a confused look.

"You moved to Colorado, went to college for four years, took out a loan, and spent the last six years of your life building a business. You did a lot of crazy things for that dream. Why is it so inconceivable that you should have to do something bold for love?"

Maybe she'd gotten a little carried away in her motivational speech. Her brother was staring at her as if he couldn't process her words. Perhaps the truth in them was sinking in.

"You're capable of moving to Wyoming," she clarified. "If the two of you are committed to each other, you can make it work."

Zach's head nodded slightly. "Maybe."

"What you mean to say is, 'Yes, wise sister, I believe you're right.'"

He laughed. "Maybe."

Joanna's happy mood began to fade. If she could convince her brother that moving across the country for love was a good idea, would he be open to the possibility that she and Aiden deserved a shot? Maybe now was the time to tell Zach about the fake relationship and Keith's unwelcome appearance.

Her shoulders sagged, and she sat back on the couch. She and Aiden weren't in love, but he was the first man she'd ever met that she could see herself falling for. She didn't meet people every day that she was instantly compatible with, and the rarity felt special. *Aiden* was special, no matter how long they'd known each other.

God sent special people into our lives when we needed them most. Even though she'd met Aiden years ago, the time hadn't been right for them. But was it even right now? There were so many odds stacked against them.

"Well, hello there."

A familiar voice grabbed Joanna's attention, and her

chin jerked up to meet Keith standing in front of her. It suddenly felt as if she were trying to breathe underwater. "Keith. Hi." Here she was stumbling over words again. Why did he always fluster her?

"This must be your brother."

Zach straightened himself in his seat. "I am. Zach Drake." He extended a hand to Keith. "Forgive my laziness. It would take some fumbling around to stand." He pointed at the crutches resting against the couch beside him.

Keith grabbed her brother's hand with a cheerful smile. "Don't bother. I heard you were here with Joanna. I've been wondering when we would get the chance to meet. I'm Keith Sanders. I work with Joanna."

Zach continued to shake Keith's hand, but his attention shifted to Joanna, no doubt wondering why she hadn't mentioned him. "Really? It's nice to meet you."

"Joanna has been so busy, I haven't gotten to spend any time with her since we've been here." Keith turned his attention to her. "Care to take a ride into town with me?"

Joanna tilted her head slightly and studied Keith. Was he seriously asking her to spend time with him after Aiden's stare down the night before? "No," she spat. "I think I already said that. Now, if you'll excuse me, I'm spending time with my brother."

Zach shoved her shoulder. "Don't let me stop you. Go have fun."

Joanna didn't look at her brother as she reiterated, lacing her words with finality. "I really can't."

"Come on," Keith pleaded. "The town has a bakery where we can get a pastry and a cup of coffee. Coffee is the only thing keeping me from freezing in this harsh weather."

The man was insistent and impossible, but she would not give in to him.

"No." Maybe short and simple was the answer.

"Jo," Zach admonished. "Ease up."

She pierced her traitorous brother with a laser stare. "I'm not going. I said no."

Keith's lips twitched as they stretched into an unnatural grin. "It's okay. Maybe later."

A man wearing a hunter-green suit jacket stepped up to Keith. "Mr. Sanders?"

"Yes," Keith answered.

"I'm Kevin Marcus, the manager here at Freedom Ridge Resort." He extended his hand to Keith. "I've been looking for you. You've been selected for a complimentary meal at Liberty Grille. Do you have a moment to speak with me about the particulars?"

Keith nodded. "Sure." He turned back to Joanna and waved. "I'll see you soon."

She bit her tongue from any further *rudeness* as Keith stepped away into the milling guests in the lounge. Aiden had mentioned he intended to let his boss know what was going on, and it seemed Kevin had been keeping a close enough eye on them to overhear her resistance to Keith's advances.

Zach shoved her shoulder as soon as her coworker was out of sight. "What was that?"

"*That* was something we need to talk about. Keith *is* my coworker. You don't see anything weird about that?"

"Why would that be weird? He seemed like a nice guy,

and he asked you to go do something fun and you snapped at him."

"He has been asking me out for weeks now, and I've said no in every way imaginable. The man doesn't know when to give up."

Zach's brows scrunched together. "Okay, don't date him, but what's the harm in going to town with him?"

Joanna sighed. Her brother wasn't seeing things in the same light as Aiden had. "He shows up here, in Colorado, at the same time I'm taking a vacation here, and says he's staying the whole month like I am. We ended up on the same vacation at the same exact time from Arizona. None of that is weird to you?"

"Maybe he heard you talking about it and thought it sounded like a good idea. I don't know. It's weird if you say it is."

Joanna stared at him as if he'd grown two heads. Where was her protective brother who bristled at the idea of her dating his friend?

"It's not a good idea if I have no interest in Keith. End of story." She didn't want to talk about this anymore.

"Okay. Okay." Zach held up his hands in surrender. "I'm sorry I said anything."

Joanna's ears burned and her breathing came quicker as Zach's dismissal settled in. How could he think she was more suited for creepy Keith than Aiden? "I think I'll take a nap before dinner. I'll meet you at the Grille at six."

"See you then. I'll just be here... doing nothing."

Joanna resisted the urge to thump her brother in the ear as she stood. She'd always been closer to Zach than her other brother, David, but right now she couldn't imagine why. Zach didn't understand her at all, and he wasn't in the mood to listen either.

Aiden had understood and stepped up to help her without being asked. He'd read her nervousness around Keith and stood beside her in an instant.

She pulled her phone from her pocket as she ascended the stairs to her room and texted Aiden.

## 14

*A*iden fell into his bed at the fire station and huffed. He hadn't realized how tired he was until his head hit the pillow. His mind had been running in circles last night and he hadn't been able to shut down to sleep. Then they'd run back-to-back calls for a child who had swallowed a key and an older man with chest pain. The day had been stacked with calls, and he hoped he could sneak in a nap.

His phone dinged in his locker, and he grunted as he retrieved it. Exhaustion sat heavy on his shoulders, but he knew better than to ignore a call. He'd seen too many family members miss the news that someone needed help to take the simple communication for granted. He had a text from Joanna and a call from Kevin.

Joanna: Thank you.

He wasn't sure what she was thanking him for, but he decided to return Kevin's call first since his boss only called him if it was important.

"Hey, boss. What's up?" Aiden sank back onto the bed.

"You were right about Keith Sanders." Kevin sounded like he was in a crowded room. Muffled voices were overlapping in the background. "I overheard him pestering Joanna today."

Aiden sat up straighter on the bed. "What did he do?" He'd had enough of Keith, and he'd just met the guy.

"He asked her to go to town with him, and she was pretty stern in her response. After the third time she refused, I stepped in and pulled him aside."

"Thanks, man. I really thought he might back off after the other night. He asked three times?"

"Yep. She must have been with her brother because they seemed to be having a silent sparring match during the whole thing. I take it he doesn't know about Keith."

Aiden sighed and let his head fall into his hand. Joanna must not have gotten a chance to talk to Zach. "I guess not."

A high voice yelled a name on Kevin's end of the call. "I have to say, I wasn't too happy with the way Keith was talking to her. If what you say is true and she's turned him down before, there was no excuse for him to approach her for a date today."

"Did he ask for a date?" If the guy thought Joanna had a boyfriend and he was still asking for a date, he had more problems headed his way.

"He just asked her to go to town with him. He mentioned the bakery."

Aiden's anger began to rise. Keith wanted to take Joanna to Aiden's mother's bakery. Not a chance. "Ha. Did you catch anything she said to Zach?"

"He told her she was being rude, but I didn't hear anything else after I pulled Keith away."

Of course it would seem like Joanna was being rude if Zach didn't know the whole story. Hopefully, she got a chance to fill him in after Keith left.

"Thanks for your help. I hate that I can't be there myself."

"No problem. I'm happy to help. I want her to feel safe here. I don't like the idea of him following her from Arizona any more than you do." Kevin had worked hard to build up a top-notch security team at the resort a few years ago. Thankfully, their services hadn't been overused.

"I appreciate it. Let me know if anything else happens."

They ended the call and he dialed Joanna's number. She answered with a groggy voice on the third ring.

"Hello."

"Were you asleep? I didn't mean to wake you." He truly didn't want to disturb her sleep, but he could admit that it was a relief to hear her voice and know she was okay.

"That's all right. I came up to the room after I got tired of hanging out with Zach."

"Yeah, Kevin told me what happened." He ended the sentence with an opening for her to tell him more.

"Thank you for putting him on notice. He was a lifesaver."

Aiden scratched his head. "I take it Zach didn't understand what was going on?"

"I hadn't mentioned anything to him. There hadn't seemed to be a good time."

"I know what you mean." He was reluctant to bring up

the subject of Joanna around his friend too. None of their conversations about her had gone well. "What happened?"

"He took the opportunity to introduce himself to Zach. Then he asked me to go to town with him. He wanted to take me to your mom's bakery." She chuckled at the coincidence.

Aiden's voice took on a flirty tone. "Did he happen to mention how your boyfriend would feel about that?"

Joanna gave a sleepy chuckle, and Aiden's heart rate sped. Even pretending to be her boyfriend lifted his spirits. The real thing might put him on cloud nine.

"I was worried he'd say something, but he didn't. That would have made the conversation with Zach even worse."

"What did he say?"

She was fully awake now and sounding like she could spit fire. "He tried to justify Keith's actions any way he could."

Aiden shook his head. "So he doesn't know I told Keith I'm your boyfriend?"

"I don't think he would have been happy to hear that, judging by his other comments, so I didn't bring it up." She rushed to add, "I'm sorry. Maybe I should have just gotten it all out in the open."

"No, I think you did the right thing. Zach isn't always open to alternative opinions. We might be fighting an uphill battle with him."

Joanna whispered, "I'm sorry."

The despair in her voice threatened to choke him. "There's nothing to be sorry for. I know he's hard to talk to sometimes. Just give him some time."

"I hope you're right."

Aiden tapped his heel in a frantic beat. "On another subject, I was wondering if you had any plans for Friday."

"Let me check my busy schedule." Joanna paused to giggle. "It looks like you're in luck. My day is wide open."

"Actually, I'm more concerned about your night plans. The Freedom Christmas parade is Friday night, and I… want to go with you." Aiden banged a fist against his forehead. He wasn't sure what he was doing. All he knew was that he wanted to be with Joanna, and she would love the Christmas parade.

"Like a date?"

"What are my options?" he asked. "Just as friends, like a date, or a real date?"

Joanna hummed. "I really want to go, and I'd like to go with you. So, let's make it one of the last two options."

Aiden stood and punched the air. After releasing his excitement, he calmed his reaction. "It's a date."

"Or like a date if Zach happens to ask. Should I drive myself?"

"On our first real date?" Aiden scoffed. "I don't think so."

She chuckled. "I meant so I don't have to worry about whether or not Zach is in the lounge to see me leaving with you. And I guess you've decided this is a real date."

"If I had my way, there wouldn't be a question."

Joanna whispered, "Me too."

Why did Zach have to be an obstacle in this one thing Aiden felt so sure about? They'd always been a team, and now it felt like their friendship was shifting.

"It'll all work out." Aiden knew it would. He'd been

praying about it, and things would work out the way they were meant to. They were just in the thick of the indecision right now.

He just hoped he would end up with Joanna when it was all said and done.

"I have to go," Joanna said, punctuating her words with a yawn. "I told Zach I'd meet him at Liberty Grille for dinner."

Someone knocked on Aiden's door. "I have to go too. Can I call you later?"

"Of course. Talk to you soon."

They ended the call and Aiden yelled, "It's open."

Carson stuck his head in and said, "Dinner. Spaghetti."

Aiden stood and pocketed his phone. "I'm in."

"Talking to your girlfriend?" Carson jested.

Aiden shrugged and his mouth lifted on one side in a controlled grin. "So what if I am?" He desperately wanted it to be true, and they *were* pretending to date—part of the time. The other times they were making a point not to show any interest in each other.

"Man, you're asking for trouble. I told you it's never going to work out with a tourist."

Aiden met Carson at the door and they made their way toward the smell of tomato sauce and garlic. "I don't care what you think. Joanna isn't just a tourist. I can't let her go or forget about her."

Carson shook his head. "You've got it bad. I don't want to be around when it all goes south. Or when *she* goes a few hundred miles south."

Aiden shoved his friend's shoulder as they entered the kitchen. "I don't need your negativity."

Carson picked up a fork and pointed it at Aiden. "You need my wisdom. You'll thank me later."

Aiden didn't want to think about what would come later. Tonight, he wanted to remember how Joanna had told him she wanted to go to the Christmas parade with him, and that was enough to override any of the odds stacked against them.

## 15

*J*oanna watched another little boy climb onto Santa's lap. Every week, the line to visit with Santa had spanned the length of the lounge, and she liked watching the kids whisper into the old man's ear.

"They're cute, aren't they?" a woman asked.

Joanna turned to see Haven, the woman she'd met when she'd first arrived. "It's fun to watch their excitement."

Haven laughed and took the seat next to Joanna on the sofa. "Except the little ones."

"Oh yeah," she laughed. "Some of those don't know what to think of the stranger with the crazy outfit. There have been many screams and lots of tears today."

Haven grinned. "Christmas has been hard for me the last few years, but this one is looking brighter. I just got married."

Joanna sat up straighter. "Congratulations! That's great news."

"It really is. I never imagined things would turn out this way. My daughter is over the moon."

"You have a daughter?"

"Miah. She's three." Haven's grin widened.

"So, is she crying at the sight of Santa this year?"

Haven's eyes widened. "I hope not. I get to bring her to work with me sometimes when my parents can't keep her, so she sees Santa here quite a bit."

"You get to bring your daughter to work? That's great."

"Yeah, my boss, Kevin, he's really good to us, and we have a daycare on site if we need it."

"I met Kevin briefly. Aiden asked him to keep an eye out for me. I've been having a little trouble with a coworker who is also visiting the lodge and doesn't know how to take no for an answer."

"Oh," Haven drawled. "You're the one Aiden has been talking about. I didn't put the pieces together. That makes so much sense."

Joanna felt a heat rise in her cheeks. "He mentioned me?"

"Mentioned you? He can't stop talking about you. We don't cross paths much, but he's been talking about you in staff meetings lately."

The heat in Joanna's face grew to a burn. "I like him. I just don't know where that leaves us when I have to go back home. I guess all I can do now is pray about it."

Haven gave her a sympathetic look. "Sometimes, that's the best thing. How did you meet Kevin?"

"He overheard Keith being pushy and diverted his attention. My hardheaded brother wasn't helping."

"I'm sorry you're having to deal with that. I'll talk to

Kevin more about it and see if we can get Heath to keep an eye out too. He's the head of security here."

"Aiden mentioned him too. I'd be grateful for any help you can give. I don't think he's dangerous, but he's persistent enough that it's worrying me."

"Oh, I understand. Say no more. We don't want him making you uncomfortable for sure."

Joanna nodded. "Keith is a coworker who followed me here, and Aiden doesn't like it one bit. He isn't taking any chances, and he told Keith he was my boyfriend the other night."

"So is Aiden your boyfriend now?" Haven asked.

"Not exactly. You see, my brother is best friends with Aiden. They've known each other since they were roommates in college, and my brother doesn't think we should be entertaining the thought of dating. In fact, he's adamantly against it."

"Why?" Haven's brows drew together. "Wouldn't he think his best friend would be good to you?"

Joanna watched a young girl hesitantly climb onto Santa's lap. "I'm not sure. The most I can figure out is that Aiden doesn't have a history of commitment, and Zach thinks that means he's incapable of a long-lasting relationship."

"But everyone has to start somewhere," Haven pointed out.

"Exactly! But there's also the fact that I live in Phoenix, and Aiden lives here."

Haven tapped her index finger against her lips. "Yeah, that's a tough one. What kind of job do you have back home? Is there a lot in Phoenix to make you stay?"

"I'm a paralegal. I've been there for a few years, and I have a great boss. I have a good reputation there." She shrugged. "My family lives there, but they didn't take it so hard when my brother moved away a few years ago."

"How many siblings do you have?"

"It's just me and my two brothers."

"Let me guess. You're the baby."

Joanna sighed. "I can't deny that one."

"Your parents might take it hard, but Phoenix isn't that far from Freedom. It's a short plane flight, and Freedom is a great place to vacation."

She had so many things to think about. Could she really move to Freedom if things worked out with Aiden? Her feelings for him were growing every day, and the forced separation was only making her want to be with him more. Aiden couldn't leave his jobs here. His skills were specialized to the cold weather.

"You're right, but it might be too early to think about moving. We're not even really dating."

Haven gave her a skeptical look. "Could have fooled me. Aiden is hung up on you."

Haven's revelation of Aiden's feelings gave Joanna a burst of hope. "He wants to go to the Christmas parade together."

"The Christmas parade is always a big hit," Haven pointed out.

"Will I see you and Miah there? I'd love to meet her."

"We wouldn't miss it. My husband, Jeremiah, will be there too." Haven's smile grew. "I'm still getting used to calling him my husband. We were best friends growing up."

"That's the sweetest! I'll keep an eye out for you at the parade."

Haven checked her watch and stood. "I have to go, but it was great talking to you again."

Joanna lifted her camera. "I think I'll take some more pictures near the fireplace. It's just so beautiful, I want to remember every inch of this place."

"You know, we have a marketing position open for the resort right now. Applications are at the front desk." She winked and lifted a hand in farewell. "See you soon."

"Thanks. See you later." The mention of a job at the resort had Joanna's heart pounding. It wouldn't hurt to read the job description, right? She could even apply for the position without any commitment. There was a chance she wouldn't even be chosen for an interview.

Her thoughts raced, and she tried her best to focus on capturing the lights and glow of the decorations with her camera. The thought of working at the resort year round was too tempting to push from her mind.

Everything was moving so fast, and her life seemed to be changing. She couldn't remember a time when she'd had so many opportunities in front of her that would change so much in her life.

Every day, she went to work, came home, slept, and went back to work the next day. Her life was a monotonous cycle, and this vacation had shaken every detail of the future she'd assumed would continue indefinitely.

Aiden and Freedom Ridge offered her a chance to live a life completely different, but was it the life she was meant to live? Could she just quit her job and move to Colorado?

She thought of Aiden and the way he'd stood up to Keith when she'd been too afraid to do it herself. Aiden had put her first, and he'd taken steps to ensure her safety when he couldn't be there himself.

Living in Colorado wouldn't be so bad. It would be wonderful with Aiden by her side.

## 16

---

*A*iden pulled his truck into the portico at the lodge, and Joanna came running out of the doors before he could shift into park. She jumped in the truck with a smile on her face and rubbed her arms.

"It's cold."

"I would have come to get you. Or at least opened your door for you."

"I know, but I'm not about to make you get out in this cold for chivalry."

Aiden shook his head and shifted into gear. He wanted to kiss that beautiful smile on her face, and he would be too tempted if he kept looking at her. "My mom would be so disappointed."

Joanna laughed. "Don't worry. I won't tell on you. Tell me about this parade. Haven said it's cool."

"The Christmas parade is a big deal in Freedom. The streets are lit up and everyone comes out to see the floats. Most businesses in town make their own and give out candy to the kids. They play Christmas music, and all of the Main Street shops are open. We have a fire engine in the parade, but I don't have to be in it. B crew is on shift right now, and C crew is riding on the engine. I'm in the A crew, so I get the night off.

Joanna leaned her elbows on the console and smiled. "I'm glad. I wouldn't have wanted to come to something like this alone. Zach isn't up to the standing yet, but he wasn't impressed with the idea from the start."

They parked in a designated lot at the end of town and walked up Main Street until the roads were blocked off. The sidewalks were already filled with people, and the parade hadn't even begun.

"Wow. The parade is serious around here." Joanna's mouth hung slightly open as she took in the bustling town.

Aiden grinned and reached for her hand. "Let's not get separated. It's crowded." People were shoulder to shoulder, and he squeezed her hand tighter, wishing her gloves weren't separating them.

They stopped at a local coffee shop for hot chocolate before finding a spot to stand on the street. Joanna's attention darted all around them as she took in the Christmas atmosphere. "This is amazing. I feel like I'm in a Christmas movie."

Aiden shrugged. "I think that's why so many families love it. Lots of people make a tradition out of it."

When the first float came into view, Joanna craned her neck to catch a glimpse. Her excitement was fun to watch, and his mind raced with thoughts of how he could recreate this joy for her. Seeing Joanna happy rivaled the thrill of a backflip on the slopes.

Children and adults alike yelled in excitement when the fire engine passed. Everyone waved at Santa and Mrs. Claus sitting on top. The chatter of kids hit an all-time high when the local animal shelter led a small group of dogs down the street.

As the parade began to die down, Aiden tossed their empty hot chocolate cups in a nearby bin and pulled Joanna to the side. They leaned against a light pole to watch families step in and out of the shops lining the busy street.

"What did you think?" he asked.

"That was so much fun! I can't believe this is such a huge event."

Aiden waved at people he knew, and a few stopped to catch up. Most of the attendees were tourists, but many of the locals had lived here with their families for generations.

His childhood Sunday School teacher, Brenda Cooper, walked by and pinched his arm with her gloved hand. "Good to see you, Mr. Clark," she said with a smile before pointing up. "You're standing under mistletoe."

Aiden and Joanna looked up at the same time, but Mrs. Cooper continued walking. Sure enough, a sprig of mistletoe was tied to the lit-up snowflake hanging from the light pole.

He lowered his head to find Joanna staring back at him. His heart beat as if he'd been running for miles. She smiled at him. Her cheeks and nose were pink from the cold, but her eyes were bright, daring him to kiss her in front of everyone in Freedom.

"I don't want this to be fake," he said. "I want to kiss

you because you're amazing and you've changed my life. Not because we're pretending to date or we're standing under mistletoe." He brushed his cold fingertips over her rosy cheek. "Can I kiss you?"

Joanna nodded and whispered, "Yes."

Aiden threaded his fingers into her hair and wrapped his other arm around her waist, bringing her body flush with his. He slowly leaned down and brushed his lips against hers. Her kiss was warm and soft in a way that had him leaning in for a deeper connection. Her arms wrapped around his shoulders, pulling him impossibly close as the busy street around them disappeared.

Holding Joanna felt more right than anything in his life. She was good for him, she was strong, and she was pushing him to be a better Christian. He wanted more of her. He needed more of her light, and he knew in that moment that he would do anything to keep her in his life.

Their kiss broke slowly, and Joanna's eyes opened. "It isn't fake, because I haven't been pretending," she confessed.

Aiden brushed a hand through her hair and kept her close. "Me either. I don't know what this means for the future, but I don't want to miss a single moment with you. I'm willing to do whatever it takes to make this work."

Joanna rested her hands on his chest. "Me too. I don't think we should ignore what's happening between us. We have some time to see how things might work out."

Aiden nodded. He wanted more than *some time*. "I know. I don't want to think about what happens when you leave. We just have to pray this is the right thing and be committed to making it work with each other."

Joanna smiled, and he leaned in, sealing his lips to hers again. The cold air and smell of chocolate and holiday spices filled his nose as he breathed in the comfort of her kiss. This was right. This was exactly what he'd been waiting for his whole life.

Joanna's hand trailed down his arm and settled into his. "Thank you for bringing me to the parade. I loved it."

Aiden looked around. The streets were beginning to clear as families made their way into shops or home to put children to bed. His eyes narrowed as he spotted a familiar face walking toward them.

He tugged on the hand Joanna held and led her into the nearest shop. "Come on. Keith is here."

Joanna followed without hesitation, and the bell above the door chimed as they slipped into Wick and Sarcasm Candle Shop. They moved to the back of the store and waited. He closed his eyes to calm his quickened breaths and racing heartbeat.

"Do you think he saw us?" Joanna asked.

"I don't think so. I doubt he would cause any trouble tonight, but I'd rather not risk him ruining our night together."

Joanna brushed her fingertips along a row of pumpkin spice candles on the shelf. "I don't think he'll find us here."

Aiden smirked. "Probably not."

She grabbed the lapels of his coat and pulled him close. Looking up at him, she whispered, "There isn't any mistletoe here."

He focused his gaze on her and closed the space between them until his lips almost touched hers. "No, there isn't, but I don't need an excuse to kiss you." Their lips met again for an intense moment that ended too soon.

Joanna's cheeks were still colored from the cold or his kiss. "We should probably buy something while we're here," she chuckled.

"Good idea."

"I think my mom would like this one." She picked it up and twisted the lid off to smell the scent. "Delicious. Apple pie. I'll ask if they can mail it to her from here."

She made her purchase and gave the shop owner the information he needed to ship the present to her mother. Aiden checked the streets for any sign of Keith before they stepped out.

"My mom's bakery is just a few blocks away," Aiden said. A lump clogged his throat at the thought of introducing Joanna to his mom, but a stronger urge was pushing him to ask her. "Would you like to meet her?"

Joanna grabbed his hand. "Lead the way."

It was a big step in their new relationship, but his mother was an important part of his life. If Joanna was committed to a relationship with him, she'd need to meet his mom while she was here. He knew they were changing the dynamic of their relationship, but the shift felt right. Aiden prayed things would work out when it came time for her to leave.

## 17

$\mathcal{T}$he night was growing colder by the minute, but Joanna didn't want to leave the beautiful Christmas town. Aiden held her close to his side with an arm around her shoulders as they made their way to the bakery where his mom worked. Excitement and the heat from Aiden's proximity kept the cold at bay, and they were stepping into Stories and Scones before she knew it. Meeting his mom should have felt like a monumental occasion, but Aiden had talked about his mom so much that Joanna felt as if she already knew the woman.

The warmth of the shop and the jingling bell welcomed them as Joanna loosened her scarf. "This place is adorable." She scanned the bakery display case and the bookshelves farther back into the store. A few readers sat in pillowy chairs at the ends of the shelves, and garlands hung along the higher shelves. "I could stay here all day."

"Mom pretty much runs the place. She loves it."

There was a line at the pastry display case, and they

took their place at the back. "I guess she doesn't know we're coming," Joanna said. "Is this a surprise she'll like?"

Aiden laughed. "Oh, she'll be thrilled."

Joanna didn't want to read too much into his comment, but her excitement got the best of her. How many women had he introduced to his mom? She picked out a chocolate-filled croissant, and Aiden had his eye on an oatmeal cream pie.

When they stepped up to the register, the cashier's jaw dropped. "There's my boy!" Her arms lifted as she trotted around the counter to hug her son. "I've missed you."

Aiden returned his mother's hug. "Sorry I haven't stopped by lately."

The woman swished her hand through the air and brushed her short hair behind her ear. "I know your friend is in town, and the Christmas season is always so busy. Still, I like to lay eyes on you every once in a while and know for sure you're all right."

Aiden turned to Joanna. "Mom, this is Joanna."

His mother covered her mouth with both hands before saying, "Oh, Aiden has told me so much about you."

"Really?" Joanna asked, surprised he'd mentioned her.

"He can't stop talking about you. I've heard stories about Zach for years, and now, his sweet sister has made her way into the picture." Aiden's mother raised her brows. "I'm Jan."

"It's nice to meet you." Before Joanna could raise her hand, Jan was hugging her like a teddy bear. The welcome was so wholesome and unexpected. It was something Joanna's own mother would do.

Jan leaned back and asked, "Will you and your brother be joining us for Christmas?"

Aiden spoke up, "I have to work at the station on Christmas day, Ma."

"You're kidding," she whined. "Well, we'll celebrate on Christmas Eve after the candlelight service."

Joanna shrugged, but she couldn't hide her smile. "I'd love to come, but let me run it past Zach. I don't think he has any plans."

"We'd love to have you," Jan said.

Aiden scratched the back of his head and grinned. "Yeah. It would be great if you could come."

"I'll be there, even if Zach isn't."

A dark-haired man stepped up beside Jan and casually slung his arm around her shoulder. "Hey, Mrs. Clark."

"Derek! It's so good to see you." Jan embraced Derek the same way she'd greeted her son.

Aiden smiled and shoved shoulders with his friend. "Joanna, this is my good friend, Derek Held. He trains search and rescue dogs."

Joanna stuck her hand out in greeting. "It's nice to meet you."

Derek took her hand. "I've heard all about you. It's nice to finally meet you too."

Joanna felt heat rushing to her cheeks. Aiden had certainly been vocal about her lately.

Jan playfully slapped Derek's arm as she gasped. "Do you have any Christmas Eve plans? I'd love it if you joined us for dinner."

"I'll try to stop by. I gave Jared the holiday off, so I might have to check in on the dogs."

"I'll save you a seat at the table." Jan smiled and turned to Aiden. "Thank you for bringing her by to meet me."

Jan bagged up their sweets and kissed her son good-bye before hugging Joanna and Derek one last time.

Aiden reached for Joanna's hand again as they stepped out of the bakery into the cold night. She wrapped her hand around his arm to gather warmth and be closer to him.

Joanna had known she would like his mom, but meeting Jan and Derek was the perfect ending to the exciting night she'd spent with Aiden. Jan was kind and friendly just like her son, and Joanna was excited to get to know Derek a little more on Christmas Eve.

Glancing up at Aiden as he walked beside her, she knew that their relationship was different. She could easily fall in love with him, and the thought had her equally elated and terrified. Aiden, his mom, and the town of Freedom were going to be hard to leave when the time came. Her life was different here, and she liked it. She hadn't checked her work email in days.

When they got back to Aiden's truck, he turned on the heat and let it idle while they warmed up.

"I liked meeting your mom and Derek. Thank you for introducing me."

Aiden smiled. "It was a treat for me too. I don't think my mom has ever met one of my girlfriends. Well, not since high school."

She removed her gloves and rubbed her hands together. "We didn't even tell her we're together."

"She'll know. I bet she'll be calling me tonight after she leaves work. I'll tell her then."

Joanna picked at her fingernails. "What are we going to do about Zach?"

Aiden brushed a hand over his scruff. "I don't know. I don't like keeping things from him, but how do you think he'll react?"

"He hasn't been very accepting of the idea," Joanna pointed out.

Aiden shifted the truck into gear and drove quietly for a while. A faint dusting of snow touched the windshield, and Joanna found herself unable to look away from the tiny flakes. Snow was something she'd always known about, but before this trip, she'd only seen it a few times in her life while visiting her brother when he attended college in Colorado.

"We'll have to tell him if he's coming to Christmas at your mom's, right?"

Aiden shrugged. "He may decide not to come."

"I just want everyone to enjoy Christmas. He's been so grouchy lately. I know it's because he's confined to the boot, but it has been so hard to talk to him lately. He doesn't want to listen."

Aiden reached for her hand and held it the rest of the way to the lodge. She focused on the feel of her hand in his, anchoring her to what was real.

Aiden was real. He'd gone above and beyond to make her feel safe and comfortable, despite her uneasiness with Keith.

Zach was also real. He'd always been there when she needed him, but now he seemed so far away. Why did it feel as if they were growing apart when she needed him most?

Freedom and the people here sure felt real, but this wasn't her life. The real world was hundreds of miles away in a high-rise in Phoenix.

She was too old to play games, but her chest ached every time she thought about a life without Aiden in it. He'd welcomed her into his without hesitation, and she wanted him to fit into her real world like a piece of a puzzle.

Aiden stopped the truck just before the portico and shifted into park. Turning in his seat to face her, he said, "I'll move closer to the door in a minute, but I wanted to say good night first."

Joanna squeezed his hand. "I had a great night, and I'm glad you introduced me to your mom."

Dim lights from the lodge entrance filtered into the cab, and the pained look on his face reinforced her own concerns. She touched the crease between his brows, gently smoothing it. He relaxed the tensed muscles and slowly wrapped his hand around the back of her neck, pulling her close. She clung to his back and breathed in the traces of his cologne.

He buried his face in the crook of her neck, and his warm breath tickled her skin as he whispered, "I want this to work. I want you to stay, but I know it's selfish of me to think it, much less say it."

Joanna's breathing hitched. "It's not selfish. I want the same things you do."

Aiden lifted his head from her shoulder and pressed his forehead to hers. "Why don't we tell him after Christmas? If we're still adamant that we both want this to work, then we tell him."

She chuckled and hoped the emotion didn't crack her voice. "You think you'll be tired of me in a few weeks?"

He dipped his head and touched his lips to hers, answering her question without a word. His movements were sweet and controlled and showed her that he could spend a lifetime adoring her without faltering.

## 18

*A*iden watched Joanna shuffle through the cold to the front entrance of the lodge. He'd intended to walk her inside, but she'd been afraid her brother might be hanging out in the lounge.

He usually spent his drive home from the resort thinking about the next day's lessons or how he could perfect a trick. Tonight, his thoughts were focused on Joanna and only served to sink his mood. They'd spent a perfect night together, but he couldn't enjoy it because the end of their time together loomed over them like a black cloud.

He'd just pulled into the driveway at his lakeside cabin when his phone rang. He answered without a hint of worry in his voice. "I was wondering when you'd call."

"I can't believe you ambushed me at work with a woman!" his mother squealed. "I needed time to talk to her, and I had to rush back to work."

Aiden chuckled as he rested the phone between his ear and shoulder to unlock the door. "I wanted you to meet her while she's still here. We don't have a lot of time."

"Oh, honey. How is this going to work? You haven't ever had a relationship with a tourist before."

"Joanna hasn't been here before. I don't know what to do." He turned on the lights and tossed his keys into a bowl near the door.

"I don't know how to help you. I can see why you're interested in her, but how serious is it?"

Aiden sighed as he flopped onto his back on the couch. "It's serious. Which means I'm all tied up in knots because I don't know how to be with her after the new year." He could handle a long-distance relationship. He'd make every effort to see her as often as possible, but would that be enough for her?

"Have you talked to her about it?" his mother questioned.

"Not much. I think we're both scared of the conversation."

Her voice grew stronger as she peppered him with questions. "Have you talked to the Lord about it?"

"That I've done. Joanna kind of set me straight when she first got here. We had a talk on one of the first nights she was here, and she encouraged me to get right with the Lord. I've had to work most weekends this month, but I'll be glad to go to the candlelight service with you."

"I'm so proud of you. I try not to pressure you because I know you'll make the right decision on your own, but you don't know how happy it makes me to hear you say that."

Aiden rubbed a hand over his face. "I'm sorry. I should

have gotten my act together sooner. It was hard for me to listen after dad died."

"Your dad is in a better place. Don't worry about him. We won't ever forget him, and he lives on in our hearts."

The familiar weight settled on his chest at the mention of his dad. "Always. I need to get to bed. I'll come see you soon."

"I love you."

"Love you too, Ma."

He ended the call and rested his arm over his eyes. The helplessness that settled over him was reminiscent of his dad's heart attack. He hadn't been able to give himself over to God's plan until recently, and maybe that's all he could do.

He took a deep breath and prayed into his quiet cabin.

"Lord, it's me again. I don't know what to do... again. I feel like I never have the answers, and maybe I'm not supposed to, but I don't want to mess this up." He swallowed the lump in his throat. "She means a lot to me, and I want to be good for her. I want it to work. I don't want to live a life just for me anymore. I want to be a man worthy of Your sacrifice. I want to be a good man for a good woman. Help me see the solution."

He fell asleep talking to the Lord and praying for guidance in his life.

THE NEXT MORNING, Aiden woke feeling rested despite sleeping the entire night on the couch. He knew he needed to step back and let God's will prevail. He would do everything he could to be with Joanna, but he knew their future rested in God's hands.

He had a full day of lessons ahead of him before dinner with Joanna and Zach. After waking up early, he made a full breakfast of bacon, eggs, and toast and still had plenty of time to stop by the lodge and talk to his boss.

On his way to Kevin's office, he spotted Heath, the chief of security at Freedom Ridge Resort. "Hey! I haven't seen you around in a while. I've been meaning to call you."

Heath was a big man with an even bigger sense of responsibility. He took his job seriously, and he was a staple at the resort who could always be counted on to help. "What's new?"

"My girlfriend is having some trouble with a guy that won't leave her alone…"

Heath held up his hands and crossed them in a T shape. "Time out. You have a girlfriend? Since when?"

Aiden scratched the stubble on his cheek. "Since last night, to tell you the truth."

Heath laughed and crossed his arms over his broad chest. "Continue."

"This guy has been asking her on dates for a few months now, and she's been saying no. Then he follows her out here from Phoenix, and he's staying here at the same place she is."

Heath's expression grew serious, and he nodded. "So, he's stalking her? Why was she in Phoenix?"

"She lives there."

Heath let his arms fall to his sides and tilted his head. "She's a tourist? Aiden, come on."

Aiden shook his head. "I don't need your lecture. I just need you to keep an eye on her if you can. Kevin had to distract the guy a few days ago when he wouldn't take no for an answer."

"I think he might have already mentioned this guy to me. Keith Sanders?"

"That's the one," Aiden confirmed.

"And your girlfriend is Joanna Drake?"

"Yep."

Heath nodded his understanding. "Apparently, Keith hasn't limited his attention to Joanna. Another guest complained about him yesterday."

"You're kidding. What a jerk."

"My thoughts exactly," Heath agreed. "I'm already on it."

"Thanks." The two men shook hands. "I owe you one."

"Don't mention it. Happy to help."

Aiden would breathe a lot easier today knowing Joanna would have help nearby if she needed it. He didn't like being away from her one bit when Keith was harassing people. It was hard to believe the guy was so stubborn after Joanna had told him she wasn't interested in him *and* she had a boyfriend.

Aiden pulled his phone from his pocket and texted Joanna on his way to the lesson.

Aiden: I can't wait to see you tonight.

Joanna's response was short and sweet, but it brought a smile to his face.

Joanna: I can't wait to see you either. Have fun at work.

He stuffed his phone in his pocket and let thoughts of seeing her later push him through the day.

## 19

*J*oanna looked at her watch and then up at the closest shop on Main Street, The Tea Cup Boutique. She sighed as she stepped up to the window display. Porcelain tea sets were displayed on staggered shelves throughout the store.

Another shop she could skip. She'd found Christmas gifts for everyone except Aiden, and the task was proving difficult. With only one week until Christmas, she needed to come up with something fast.

She'd been shopping in Freedom for hours, but nothing had jumped out at her yet. She wanted Aiden's gift to be special. *He* was special, and she wanted to show him that she'd put a lot of thought into his gift.

The problem was that all the thinking of the last few days hadn't brought her closer to a decision. She'd even considered asking her brother for help but decided that was probably just asking for trouble. She could stop by Stories and Scones and talk to Jan, but she didn't want to distract her at work.

Joanna's phone rang in her coat pocket and she pulled off one glove to answer. A grin spread on her face as she accepted the call. "I was just thinking about you."

"Really?" Aiden asked. "I was thinking of you."

She rubbed her frozen cheeks with her gloved hand. Hearing his voice sent a tingle up her spine. "Good thoughts I hope."

Aiden chuckled. "Always. What are you up to?"

"Shopping for your Christmas gift in town."

"Ha! I already got your gift. I always win Christmas."

Interesting. They'd only been "officially" seeing each other for a few hours. "I didn't know Christmas was a competition."

"Of course it is. I give the best gifts."

Joanna rolled her eyes and chuckled. "How in the world did you have time to get me something already?"

"I got it before you agreed to be my *real* girlfriend. Even pretend boyfriends should dote on their girlfriends at Christmas."

"Remind me to thank your mom the next time I see her."

"For raising me right? I can't get the credit for this one?"

"Of course you do. You're the sweetest." He truly was. He was in the thick of the busiest season and still making time for her at every turn. "What are you doing?"

Wind whipped on Aiden's side of the call. "Taking a break during a lesson. I can't wait to see you tonight."

"I can't wait to see you too." She just hoped having dinner with Zach and Aiden wasn't a bad idea. "We'll meet you at the Grille at six."

"Can't wait. Be careful today. I asked my friend, Heath, to keep an eye out for Keith too, but he's not with you in town."

"I know. I'm staying alert." It was nice of Aiden to take her unease regarding Keith as seriously as she did. Her own brother had dismissed her concerns. "Thanks for looking out for me."

"Always. I have to go. See you soon."

"Bye." She disconnected the call and realized she'd walked all the way down Main Street and back up the other side to Zach's car.

Feeling defeated, she drove back to the resort with her mind searching for a gift for Aiden. She hadn't come up with anything by the time she shut off the car in the parking garage. Keeping an eye out for Keith, she took the elevator to the main floor and tried to hurry through the lounge to the stairs. The less time she spent in public, the better.

"Miss Drake?"

Joanna jumped at the unfamiliar male voice behind her. Covering her heart as if it would settle the rhythm, she said, "Yes. I'm Joanna Drake."

The tension in her shoulders eased when she realized he was wearing a security uniform. He was tall and broad, but his demeanor was friendly.

"I'm Heath. Aiden spoke with me about a problem you've been having."

His expression was serious, but his eyes were kind. Aiden said Heath was a friend, and she trusted Aiden's judgment.

"Yes, Aiden mentioned you."

Heath pulled a card from his front shirt pocket. "Here is my number in case you need anything when Aiden isn't around. We've had some issues with Mr. Sanders that extend beyond your complaints, and we're not taking the situation lightly."

"That's awful. I reported his actions to the human resources department at the firm where we both work, but they didn't seem concerned."

Heath's brow furrowed. "He's been hanging around the lounge a lot today. Please be cautious."

Joanna held up the card he'd given her. "Thank you, Heath. I appreciate your help." She looked around, suddenly feeling watched and vulnerable. "I think I'll spend the rest of the day in my room."

"A wise choice." He tipped his chin to her. "Merry Christmas."

"Merry Christmas to you too."

Her heart raced in her chest as she tried to take the stairs at a normal pace instead of running from the watching eyes the way she wanted. In the hallway leading to her room, she looked over her shoulder no less than six times before reaching Zach's door and knocking.

Her brother's muffled, "Coming," was followed by silence for what seemed like ten minutes before he opened the door. "Hey, Jo."

"Hey. I just wanted to let you know I'm back from town."

Zach jerked a thumb over his shoulder. "Want to watch *Home Alone*?"

"Thanks, but I have some internet shopping to do."

He shrugged. "Suit yourself. I'll just be here reliving my childhood."

"I'll come by before dinner."

"See you."

Zach closed the door, and Joanna unlocked her own a few rooms down the hall. Still looking over her shoulder, she slipped inside and flipped the latch at the top of the door. The card Heath had given her was still in her hand and she slipped it into an interior pocket of her purse.

Settling on the bed with her laptop, she checked work emails, which led to an hour of replies and phone calls. Then she began a search for a gift for Aiden she could have shipped to the resort by Christmas. Many possibilities she ran across weren't offering shipping so close to the holiday, but she finally found a gift she thought he would love and paid extra for express shipping.

She exported the most recent photos from her camera to her laptop and sent a few of the best ones to Aiden. He'd expressed interest in her photographs a few weeks ago and asked her to send them to him. Since then, she made a point to email him a few every day showcasing the beautiful place he called home.

There wouldn't ever be enough photos to do Freedom justice. The beauty of this place always stunned her and often led her to a prayer of thanks for the chance to see it. She especially loved the way the sun reflected off the snow or cast beautiful colors in the clouds above the peaks.

Her phone rang beside her, startling her as it pierced the quiet room.

"Hello."

"Hey, how's the vacay going?" Brandi asked.

Joanna studied another breathtaking photo. "Amazing. This place is like a whole other world."

"It *is* another world. Not yours."

Brandi's dose of realism stung Joanna's good mood. "I was just going through my photos from today. Want me to send you some?"

"Yes, please. I may never see real snow."

"It's so cold here. Like, freeze your insides cold." Joanna shuddered at the mention of the frigid temperatures.

"Sounds lovely," Brandi jested. "How's the cranky brother?"

"He's fine. Not quite as cranky if I give him plenty of space. Or maybe I'm just not around enough to hear his grumblings. What are you up to?"

"Nothing," Brandi dramatically huffed. "I'm bored without you."

"What about the Christmas parties?"

"Exhausting. When did I get too old to have fun?"

Joanna clicked send on the email to Brandi. "When you turned thirty."

"Shut up. Don't rub it in that you have plenty of good years left."

Joanna sighed. "Thirty isn't old, and you know it. It's not like you're a spinster."

"How is Aiden?" Brandi asked, changing the subject.

"Pretty good. I just ordered his Christmas present online."

"What? You're getting him a gift?"

"He said he wants to be more than my fake boyfriend."

Joanna wouldn't get tired of telling people that Aiden Clark was her new boyfriend.

"Stop it," Brandi said. "He didn't."

Joanna smiled. "He did. Last night at the Christmas parade."

"I can't believe you're living in a Hallmark movie. It's not fair."

"Does that mean there will be a happily ever after?" Joanna asked wistfully.

"Do you know what you're going to do?" Brandi's concern was thick in her voice.

Joanna rubbed her forehead. "No. I know I really like him, but we don't have a lot of time together. I even met his mom last night."

Brandi whistled. "You're in trouble. I wouldn't want to be you."

"Thanks for the support," Joanna grumbled.

"Hey, I have to run. Mom is here. I'll call you later."

Joanna ended the call with the looming threat of her departure hanging over her. She had two weeks left in Freedom, but it didn't seem like enough. She'd already been able to spend over a month on vacation at Christmas. It was selfish to still want more.

Lying back on the bed, she closed her eyes and focused on calming her breathing. "Lord, why am I so conflicted? I feel like Aiden came into my life for a reason, but I'm not sure what that is yet. Am I even on the right path?" She laid the back of her hand over her eyes. "Show me the way You want me to go, Lord. I'm lost." Her words were barely a whisper, but they cracked on her emotion.

She'd tossed and turned the night before, unable to

sleep with the indecision warring inside her heart. Praying had been the only thing to quiet her mind long enough to allow sleep to take her, and the same happened now as she asked for guidance and understanding once again.

## 20

$\mathcal{A}$iden changed out of his snowboarding gear and cleaned up in the staff lockers in record time. He always had fun on the slopes, but he was ready to lay eyes on Joanna. With Keith around, he didn't like being away from her.

He stepped into the lounge, tugging on his collar with five minutes to spare. Scanning the room for Joanna and Zach, he spotted her blonde hair near the huge fireplace close to the entrance to the restaurant and headed that way.

Zach was actually smiling, which was a good sign, and he greeted Aiden with a pat on the shoulder. They were friends, and he needed to remember that they looked out for each other.

"Hey, how are the slopes?"

Aiden scrunched up his nose. "Cold and windy. You'd hate it."

Zach went in for a full-on hug. "You're the best."

Aiden shoved his friend away with a laugh and turned to Joanna. "Hey. What have you been up to?"

She narrowed her eyes at him in a flirtatious look. "Just shopping."

"Find anything that caught your eye?" Aiden asked.

Her gaze locked with his, and he couldn't look away. Zach wasn't stupid, but Aiden was powerless against the hold Joanna had on him.

"Nothing in town."

The hostess gestured for them to follow her into Liberty Grille. They took their seats at a table near the expansive windows, and Zach touched Joanna's arm to catch her attention. She hadn't looked away from the mountains beyond the windows.

"Hey, I meant to ask if you'd mind driving me to the doctor on Monday. I think they'll tell me I can give up the boot."

"Sure," Joanna said. "Will you be able to snowboard?"

He studied his menu. "I'm not sure. I don't want to think about the possibility that they could say no."

"I have to work at the station tomorrow and Monday, and I promised Mom I would spend some time with her," Aiden said. "Maybe we could all go on Wednesday if they clear you." He turned to Joanna, hoping he could keep his intense interest in her at bay. "Would you be up for that?"

Zach rolled his eyes. "Realistically, I might be practicing beginner moves when I do get a chance to go, so maybe it's a good time to introduce you to the thrill of snowboarding."

"Sounds like fun. Can I rent the things I'll need?"

Aiden nodded. "We have everything in the rental shop

here. I'll walk down there with you after dinner and get everything set up."

*This must be a dream.* Seeing Joanna in snowboarding gear might be the highlight of his year.

"Was that a jab at me?" Zach jested, pointing to his crutches.

"Dude, you can hobble with us if you want."

Zach waved away the offer. "I plan to crash after we eat. Sitting around all day watching movies is exhausting."

The waiter stepped up to the table and took their drink orders. Zach gave his opinion of every item on the menu at the Grille and every drink at Mountain Mugs since he'd been able to try them all while confined to the lodge. Joanna told Zach about the shops in town, and Aiden watched her eyes light up as she described the things she'd seen.

Growing up in Freedom sometimes kept Aiden from seeing the beauty in it. It was his everyday life, and it was easy to forget about the joy others found in visiting a new place.

"Did you see the lion and lamb statue on Third?" he asked.

"Yes! It's beautiful." Joanna turned to Zach. "You have to try the chocolate-filled croissants at Stories and Scones Bakery. They're so good." Joanna gave Aiden a questioning look before continuing. "Aiden's mom is the manager. You'd love her."

What was she doing? Was she ready to tell Zach about the relationship? His throat went dry. She'd set it up well, and it would be a relief to get it out in the open.

"You know her?" Zach asked.

Joanna brushed her hair behind her ear. The nervous gesture drew the attention of everyone at the table. "I met her at the Christmas parade."

"With Aiden?" Zach turned his attention to Aiden.

"I told you everyone goes to the Christmas parade." Aiden was working hard to look casual, unsure of where this would lead them.

Zach furrowed his brow, and just as his mouth opened to speak, Joanna rested a hand on his arm.

"She invited us to the candlelight service at church and to her house for dinner on Christmas Eve. I thought that was very nice of her since we aren't spending the holiday with our own family."

Zach stared at her for a moment before nodding. "Yeah. That is nice. We should go."

And Aiden could breathe again. Joanna had completely changed the course of the conversation. They still hadn't revealed their relationship to Zach, but maybe it was best to use baby steps.

"Good. I already picked up a gift for her in town," Joanna said as the waiter brought their orders.

The conversation shifted to snowboarding as they ate, and Aiden was glad for the break. Telling Zach about his relationship with Joanna wouldn't be easy, but surely he could see how well they worked together.

After dinner, Aiden ran through a list of equipment they would be looking for with Joanna while Zach gestured to the elevator.

"I'll catch you two later. *Christmas Vacation* is coming on again tonight."

Joanna wrapped her arms around her brother's neck. "I thought you watched that last week."

"I did. The Christmas movies are getting me into the holiday spirit."

Chuckling, she released him. "Have fun, and call me if you get bored."

"Ring, ring," Zach joked before hobbling into the open elevator. "Catch you later."

When the doors closed, Aiden released a heavy breath. "That was nerve-wracking."

"Tell me about it. I thought we might have a chance to tell him, but he didn't seem open to the idea, so I bailed."

Aiden wrapped his arms around her and kissed the top of her head. "You were amazing."

"Thanks. I hope Christmas Eve isn't that stressful. I'm not sure how much more of that I can stand."

He'd been weighing the risks versus the rewards of telling Zach before Christmas Eve, but after tonight's dinner, it might be best to stick to the plan to tell him after the holiday. "I think it'll be okay. Mom is great at keeping the conversation where she wants it to be. I don't think he would say anything in front of her." Taking her hand, he led her to the outdoor equipment shop.

"You're right. By the way, how did I get roped into snowboarding? I need to warn you that Zach got all the coordination in the family."

Aiden laughed and held the door open for her to enter the shop. "Don't worry. I'll take care of you. And if you decide you're not up to it, we can always call it a day early."

She shook her head. "I'm not a quitter. We're doing this."

Her determination brought a smile to his face that didn't fade as he fitted her for gear and explained the use of each item. She listened intently and asked dozens of questions. He had a feeling they would continue over the next few days. She had an immersive personality and caught on quickly.

They reserved everything she would need for Wednesday within the hour. The night was inky black through the windows as they stepped out of the shop and back into the lounge.

"Do you have to go?" Joanna asked.

Aiden grinned and pulled her close to his side. When she looked up at him with those pleading eyes, he wanted to bend to her every wish. "Not yet. You have something in mind?"

She pointed toward the door. "Want to sit by the fire pit?"

Cuddling up to Joanna on a cold night sounded like a perfect ending to a long day. "Always."

Joanna pulled her jacket tighter around her middle as they walked to the closest pit. He moved a chair a little closer and gestured for her to sit in his lap. She sat with her legs on one side of his and leaned into his chest. With his arms wrapped around her in the quiet night, he could almost forget the challenges that lay ahead of them.

"For someone who hasn't been too forgiving of the frigid weather, you sure do spend a lot of time outside," Aiden whispered.

"It's not so bad," she admitted. "Especially when you're keeping me warm."

Aiden nuzzled his nose against her neck. "Is that all I'm good for? Keeping you warm."

She turned her face slightly so that their mouths lined up, and the intensity of her gaze stole his breath.

"No. You're so much more," she whispered against his lips.

He captured her words with his mouth, breathing them, taking them in and letting them find a home in his heart. She was more than he'd ever expected. She was kind, selfless, and loving.

She was love—the kind he'd never known until it became a part of him that he recognized and could call by name.

He loved her, and it would make losing her unbearable.

## 21

*J*oanna's phone dinged on the bed beside her, waking her from a light sleep. The TV was still on, and Zach was stretched out on the other bed. They'd both dozed off in his room while watching *A Charlie Brown Christmas*.

Rubbing her eye with one hand, she picked up her phone with the other. Emails, and lots of them, lit up her phone. She'd been avoiding them for days, and now was as good a time as any to catch up.

The newest email in her inbox caught her eye first. Her recent order had been delivered.

She snuck a glance at Zach, snoozing away, and eased from the bed. Careful not to wake him, she snuck out of the room and jogged down the stairs. Aiden's Christmas gift had arrived, and she couldn't wait to see it.

She made her way to the check-in desk in the lobby and waited in line behind a couple checking in. Joanna scanned the lounge. It was teeming with people. Freedom Ridge Resort gained guests by the day as the week of

Christmas arrived, and now she understood why. Everything about this place was beautiful.

When it was her turn, she stepped up to the desk and gave the employee a big smile. "Hi, I'm Joanna Drake. I received an email saying a package had arrived for me."

The man disappeared into a back room, and Joanna rested her elbows on the counter to wait.

"There you are."

Her head jerked up at the unwelcome, familiar voice. "Keith."

His smile was strained, but his tone sounded as even and casual as usual. "I've been looking all over for you. Are you avoiding me?"

The slight reprimand in his words told her to tread carefully. She swallowed and cleared her throat. "I've been busy." She looked to the door that led to the staff room behind the check-in desk and prayed the man would return soon. Could she catch the attention of the other worker behind the desk?

"I know. You're impossible to find. It's not like this place is *that* big." Keith gripped her elbow. "Let's get out of here. I want to spend some time with you."

Joanna jerked her arm, but his grip held firm. "Let go of me. I don't want to go anywhere with you." Her voice rose as the extent of his strength became apparent. His slim frame was deceiving.

"I've been hanging out here for almost a month trying to catch you, and I'm sick of it." His brows furrowed as he leaned closer to her, still holding her elbow. "Stop dodging me."

Her pulse beat hard, and a roaring filled her ears as

panic set in. She wasn't leaving here with him. "I have a boyfriend, and I wouldn't go anywhere with you even if I didn't."

Keith scoffed. "I'm not worried about him. He lives here, and you belong in Phoenix." He looked around as if he wanted to spit at the elaborate decorations. "We both belong in Phoenix."

"Keith, I said let go of me. Now!" She was almost screaming as the fear of what he would do settled in.

People were starting to look their way, their attentions drawn as she began to cause a scene. Good. She wanted them to witness this. He'd been trying to get her to leave with him, and her chest constricted in fear when she thought of what he might do if he ever did get her alone.

The man reappeared from the back room. "Miss Drake. Here you go."

Keith released her elbow unceremoniously, and she reached for the package. "Thank you." If he only knew how thankful she was for his interruption.

"Is mister, um, Kevin around?" She wasn't sure of Kevin's last name, but the man might fetch the manager in a hurry if he assumed she wanted to make a complaint.

"I'll page him right away, Miss Drake." The man picked up a phone beside him.

Joanna turned back to Keith with a scowl on her face. "You need to leave. You need to stop harassing me, and leave me alone. I'll report you if you so much as talk to me again." Her voice sounded much stronger than she felt.

Keith narrowed his eyes at her and cast a glance back at the man on the other side of the counter as if he were weighing his options.

She straightened her back in an attempt to bring herself up to his height. "He's calling the manager. I suggest you leave before he gets here. I won't hesitate to tell him that you're bothering me."

Keith's nostrils flared, and he stormed off without a backward glance.

Joanna released a heavy breath and leaned over the counter. "Can you please tell him it's Joanna Drake, Aiden's friend?"

"Yes, Miss Drake."

She turned her attention to the crowd around them. There were so many people, and she was exhausted from keeping an eye out for Keith all the time.

A familiar uniform caught her eye, and she waved a hand to catch the man's attention. "Heath."

He spotted her and hurried his steps toward her. "Miss Drake. How can I help you?"

Boy, was she happy to see him. Her gaze darted to the left and then the right. "Keith was just here, and he was very pushy. He grabbed my elbow and wouldn't let go when I asked him to." She rubbed the elbow, remembering the grip he'd held on her. "He pretty much said he wasn't afraid of Aiden, and he was angry that I've been avoiding him."

"I'll make sure Kevin and Aiden know. I've let the other security guards know too. He shouldn't touch you like that."

Joanna nodded. "I think I may have really underestimated him. He seemed furious just now. I asked this man to see if he could find Kevin."

"Can you stick around and wait for him? I want him to

hear this, especially since he's been bothering other guests."

"Of course," Joanna agreed. "Did you say guests?" How many other women had he treated this way? A chill ran down her spine as she wondered if there had been women who hadn't been brave enough to speak up or hadn't had anyone to help them.

Kevin arrived, straightening his suit jacket. His pace was quick as he met them at the desk. "What happened?"

"Keith was here, and he isn't happy that I've been avoiding him. He grabbed my arm and wouldn't let go when I told him to. He was really angry."

Kevin's frown deepened. "Where did he go?"

"I'm not sure," Joanna said. "I didn't pay attention to where he went."

Kevin turned to Heath and crossed his arms over his chest. "What can we do about him?"

"I'll check and see if he has a record or any warrants. In the meantime, we need to keep an eye out for him, and I think Joanna should stay out of sight."

Joanna held up her hands in surrender. "You don't have to tell me twice. I'll hang out with my brother in his room until Aiden's shift at the station is over."

Kevin nodded. "Good. I'll let the front desk workers know what's going on."

Joanna turned to Heath and paused for a moment as an idea came to her. If Keith wasn't backing down, she needed to be one step ahead of him. "Would you do me a favor?"

## 22

*A*iden wrung his hands on the steering wheel as he drove the salted roads toward Freedom Ridge. His days with Joanna were slipping away, and he wanted to spend every available minute with her.

His eagerness to have her in his sight and in his arms was two-fold. Soon, she wouldn't be here to laugh with him, touch his face when they kissed, or give him that playful glance that had his heart racing. He wanted to record his moments with her in his memory and play them on repeat when they were apart.

But he also wanted that menacing Kcith to know that he had no right to push her around. If Aiden ever saw the man again, he'd lay down the law about harassing Joanna.

He was fed up with her coworker's misplaced entitlement. The man needed a wakeup call, and Aiden would be more than happy to be the rooster. He should have put his foot down the first time he'd met the guy, but Joanna had been understandably cautious.

Stopping his truck just before the entrance to the

lodge, he quickly shifted into park. Joanna burst through the door and ran to him, a heart-stopping smile covering her face.

He hopped out of the truck and met her in front, wrapping her in his arms and lifting her off her feet to twirl her in a circle. The smell of black cherry and vanilla filled his senses as he buried his face in her hair. She clung to his back, and he tightened his hold on her. Any tension he'd built up worrying on the way to pick her up melted away once she was in his arms.

"I missed you," she whispered. "I know that's silly because I just saw you, but—"

"But every minute feels important right now," Aiden finished. They had so little time left together, and he'd become conscious of every moment spent away from her.

Joanna leaned back and rested her gloved hands on his cheeks. "It is important. You're important."

Aiden's breath hitched. How could she be the one? Why was this kind, amazing, beautiful woman leaving in just over a week? He didn't want a relationship with her that had an expiration date. He wanted an infinite number of days and nights with her by his side.

He loved her. He was sure of it. No matter how strong her feelings were for him, he knew the truth of his own. He pulled her back into the embrace and let his heart beat against hers where it was meant to stay.

He cleared his throat. "Are you ready to snowboard?"

Joanna was all smiles. "As ready as I'll ever be."

They met Zach inside and fitted Joanna with her rental gear. They were on the slope within the hour. Zach showed Joanna how to get comfortable with the board while he tested out his own ankle. Once he was satisfied that his ankle was stable, Zach moved on to some more complex moves while Aiden hung back to give Joanna a beginner lesson.

She was a fast learner, but the main factor working against her was endurance. She wasn't used to physical exertion in negative temperatures. Snowboarding was a marathon, not a sprint. If it wasn't the use of a wide range of muscles that usually sat dormant for beginners, it was the altitude. After a few hours, he could tell her energy was waning.

They'd stayed at the top of the slope most of the day and took the gondola back to the lodge around lunch.

Zach tested his range of motion on the way down, rolling his ankle in every direction. "I think it held up okay today. I don't know if I'll get to go all out on it before I leave, but it's better than nothing."

Joanna elbowed her brother in the side. "Better safe than sorry."

"Oh, don't worry. I'm sorry enough. Looking out the windows these last few weeks has been torture."

The whole day had been perfect hanging out with Joanna and Zach. Aiden wanted to stick around, but he had some errands to run. Joanna had agreed to come to dinner at his house tonight, and he wanted everything to be ready. "I need to get on the road. I'll catch up with you later."

Zach whined, "Don't leave me. I'll be bored without you."

Joanna stuck her hands on her hips. "I'm standing right here."

Zach cupped a hand around the wrong side of his mouth and stage whispered to Aiden, "She makes me watch *Cake Boss*."

She threw her hands in the air. "What's wrong with *Cake Boss*?"

Aiden smiled at the siblings. When they were in college together, Zach had always talked about how his sister annoyed him endlessly. Now, Aiden knew the truth of it. Zach was the instigator.

Aiden laid a heavy hand on his friend's shoulder. "I've seen every episode of *Cake Boss*. I watch it with my mom when I visit."

With narrowed eyes, Zach spat, "Traitor."

Aiden shook his head as he turned to leave. "See you later." He'd be seeing Joanna later today when he picked her up for their date, but Zach didn't need to know that. He'd probably be too busy watching the Hallmark Channel to know she was gone.

AIDEN SMILED as Joanna ran for his truck. It was the second time today she'd been eager to greet him, and he knew he was getting spoiled to her welcoming smiles.

"Let's get you warmed up." Aiden led her to the passenger side of his truck. After closing the door behind her, he slowly walked around the truck to his side, letting the freezing cold air distract his thoughts from the sobering reality waiting for them.

Joanna was smiling and wiggling in her seat in an

attempt to warm up when he got in. "I can't wait to see where you live."

Aiden grinned and shifted into gear. She admired the scenery the entire drive. The snow was beautiful, covering everything in a thin blanket of white.

He made the last turn beneath the frozen pines into his driveway. It took every ounce of restraint he possessed to keep from checking her reaction.

Once he'd parked in front of the modest cabin he called home, he turned to her without shutting off the engine. "Well, this is it."

Joanna had bitten her lips between her teeth as she stared wide-eyed.

"What do you think?"

Joanna slowly shook her head. "There's no way you live here."

Aiden laughed. "Yep. That's my little cabin." It could have been smaller. It was a two-bedroom with a wrap-around porch that overlooked the small frozen lake directly before them.

"Aiden, it's perfect." She put her hands on her cheeks. "It looks like it belongs in Freedom, if that makes any sense."

"What do you mean?"

"Everything here is so beautiful it's breathtaking. It makes me stop and stare at the amazing world that the Lord created for us. I'm just in awe of it all."

Aiden turned to the lake spread out before them. Snow covered its banks, and the moon cast a silvery blue over the ice.

"I've been so busy that I forgot to appreciate what's

around me," Joanna said. "It's easy to get swept up in the fast pace of the city. I never notice anything, much less how beautiful nature can be."

Aiden took her hand and lifted it to his mouth. He placed a kiss on her wrist at the edge of her glove. "Let's go inside, and I'll show you around."

They moved quickly through the windy night and into the cabin. Aiden flipped on the lights as they entered and took her coat.

"I love it," Joanna said.

Aiden pushed up his sleeves and took her hand, leading her to the kitchen. "You want me to show you around before we eat?"

"Of course."

He gestured to the main room. The first floor had an open floor plan with the kitchen and dining area. "I'm not much for decorating, so it's pretty minimal around here."

Joanna squeezed his hand. "It doesn't need anything extra." The plank walls were broken up by windows looking out over the lake.

He showed her around the main floor before leading her upstairs. There were two bedrooms, but one had a higher view of the lake he knew she would love.

Standing with her hands propped on the windowsill, she chuckled. "And to think that you work so much, you probably don't spend any time here."

Aiden leaned against the doorframe with his arms crossed over his chest. "It's not work if you love what you do. I have some pretty good views from the ridge too, and the fire station keeps me on my toes."

She stood as still as a statue looking out over the lake. "It's so quiet out here."

Aiden stepped behind her and pointed down the bank to the right. "There are a few other cabins on the lake, but you can only see one from here. I like the privacy and quiet after the hustle of work and the town during the day, especially at Christmastime."

She turned to him, a breath away from brushing her lips against his cheek, and whispered, "I know this is a busy time for you, and I know what it means that you've made so much time for me."

Aiden barely moved his face a fraction of an inch to face her. He could feel her warm breath on his mouth. "I want to be with you all the time," he whispered.

Joanna's breath hitched as she breathed in. A heavy moment settled between them as she whispered, "We should probably get started on dinner before we end up making out in your bedroom."

His brow furrowed at her nervousness as he laid his hand out, palm up, between them.

She eyed it for a moment before placing her hand in his where he wrapped it up in both of his.

"I know Keith has made you uncomfortable, but I don't want you to ever feel that way around me." Pressing his lips hard to hers, he left them there for two heartbeats before pulling away and staring into her dark-brown eyes. "Let's go have dinner."

Her mouth turned up in a grin that she tried to contain. "I'll help."

∼

Cooking dinner beside Joanna was a lot more exciting than he'd expected it to be. They made a game of brushing past each other and stealing silent kisses. She knew a lot about cooking, which surprised him. Apparently, she made a dish every Wednesday night for potluck at her church, and there was a standard to live up to since she was one of the younger women in the congregation.

"Are you missing your family?" he asked as he set the table.

"Yeah. Christmas was always a big deal at our house. With two brothers, it was also loud and crazy."

Aiden laughed. "My Christmases are a lot quieter. It's just me and my mom." His mom would be thrilled to have Joanna and Zach around to celebrate with them this year. His mother had always been a friendly, social person, and the calm Christmases with just Aiden—now that his dad was gone—were quiet and somber.

He watched Joanna moving through his small kitchen as if she belonged there and wondered what future Christmases would be like compared to this one. It was a time of year to celebrate the birth of the Savior, and he wanted to spend it with Joanna every year.

Next year would pale in comparison to this one if Joanna weren't still in his life. On the other hand, if they were able to work things out between them, he could be looking at a future full of wonderful Christmases together.

Joanna stepped up behind him and wrapped her arms around his middle, linking her hands on his stomach. "My mom and dad always read us the story of Jesus's birth on Christmas Eve and let us open one present."

"You'll get to open my present for you on Christmas Eve at Mom's house. And we usually read the same thing either at church or at home."

She rested the side of her face against his back. "I know. That's what makes it so special. I'm not with my family this year, but I don't feel like I'm missing out."

He rubbed his hand over hers and prayed that the Lord would allow him to keep Joanna in his life. He wanted to give her everything she wanted, and she was too special to lose.

## 23

"You get five stars for this dinner," Joanna said around the bite she chewed.

Aiden leaned over the table on his elbows, relaxing into the conversation with her. "Is that five out of ten or five out of five?"

"Five out of five."

He grinned back at her. "You mean *we* get five stars. I had help."

Joanna slumped back in her chair and admired the view of the moonlit lake. "What did your family do for the holidays? Did you have any fun traditions growing up?"

Aiden looked around as if searching for a memory in the room with them. "It's not really a tradition, but my parents always danced at Christmas."

Joanna sat up, intrigued by the concept. "What do you mean?"

He pulled his phone from his pocket and tapped a few times. "My mom and dad were the perfect couple. If they ever got mad at each other, they never let me hear it."

The soothing voice of a woman began to sing "Auld Lang Syne" from Aiden's phone. He stood and extended his hand to her with a mischievous twinkle in his eye. "May I have this dance?"

Joanna's breath hitched at the sweetness of his gesture. She took his hand and stood, unsure of what else to do, and excited about the prospect of doing something new.

Aiden pulled her close and rested a hand on her lower back. "We used to all put up the decorations together, and we had a music box that played half a dozen Christmas songs. It played through the evening, and Mom and Dad would forget the decorations and dance. On Christmas morning, they never worried about a mess or anything else they could get caught up in that day. They mostly danced."

She let the lull of the music wrap her in peace as she settled into Aiden's arms. Could she dare to imagine a Christmas in her future when she and Aiden would tell the story of Christ's birth to their kids and dance in the glow of the colorful lights?

He rested his cheek on her head. "That first Christmas with Mom after Dad died was awful. She cried the whole time." Aiden cleared his throat. "It was one of the only times she let me see her grief. So I danced with her."

Joanna squeezed her eyes closed against the sadness. She couldn't imagine losing someone so close to her. "I'm sorry."

"Now, Mom and I dance at Christmas, and she doesn't cry. I think it helps her remember him."

They danced through the remainder of the song in silence. It was over too soon, and they didn't step away from each other. Instead, they continued to dance, reluctant to let the end of the song or her time here pull them apart.

"Can we sit outside?" Joanna asked.

Aiden held her hand and led the way, grabbing a wool blanket from the couch as they passed. A stationary bench swing took up one end of the porch, and they sat close beneath the blanket, burrowing from the freezing December night.

"You have the best view here," Joanna whispered, unwilling to disturb the peace around them.

Aiden pulled her closer with his arm around her. "I know I should be enjoying every second of time we have together, but I can't stop thinking about what happens when you have to go."

She sat up straighter and faced him, ready to meet their fate head on. "What do you want to happen?"

Aiden's expression was serious as he brushed a hand over her cheek. "I want to be with you. I want to make this work. If you still want me, I'll do anything to make you happy."

She blinked hard, unsure if the urge came from the cold wind or the moisture building in her eyes. "I want that too. What do we do?"

Aiden's green eyes reflected the silver moonlight as he said, "I love you. I know you might not know what that means to me, but it's—"

Joanna placed a finger over his lips, interrupting him. The words on her heart burst from her lips. "I love you too. I *do* know what it means, and I know everything is going to work out."

He reached for her hand stilling his words and wrapped it in his own. "We don't have to figure everything out now, but now that we know we're both in this together…"

"We won't have to worry about the end. We can just enjoy the moment."

Aiden nodded. "I love you so much. You've filled a lot of pieces in my life that I've been missing. I didn't know I needed someone until you showed up. I wasn't thinking about fixing my relationship with the Lord until you urged me to think about it. I'm just trying to say that I'm thankful you've changed me, for the good."

He lowered his face to hers, pulling her closer with a gentle hand wrapped around her nape. His lips met hers and whispered promises without words. They conveyed his vow to her, that he would fight for the life they could have together.

With each movement, she met his covenant match for match, building the bond that would forever tie them to each other.

When the kiss ended, neither wanted to break the silence. She rested her head on his shoulder and watched the reflection of the moon on the nearby lake. She let the lulling rock of the swing and the tingle of Aiden's fingertips circling on her palm lead her into sleep in his arms.

The ringing of her phone jarred both of them out of contentment. She fumbled for it in her pocket. Lifting it in front of her face, she blinked rapidly to adjust her vision to the bright light in the darkness.

"It's Zach. And it's after nine o'clock." Joanna sighed. "He's probably wondering where I am."

"We should get you back to the lodge."

"What do I tell him?"

It seemed like they didn't have much of a choice. "Maybe we should talk to him tonight. None of this is going to change, and he needs time to get used to it."

Declining the call, she opened the message app on her phone.

Joanna: Be there soon.

She took a deep breath and stood. The shock of the cold hit her like knives after the warmth of the blanket and Aiden's arms.

He took her hand as they walked to his truck. "Don't worry. I'm right beside you."

AIDEN PARKED in an employee lot on the side of the lodge. The colorful Christmas lights could be seen through the windows of the lounge. Her heart beat like a hammer in her chest as she approached the entrance, but Aiden reached for her hand, and the beating calmed.

Zach was waiting for them in the lounge. He sat straight backed in a chair nearest the entrance and jumped to his feet when he saw them.

"Where have you been? I thought you were in your room, but..." His gaze cut to Aiden, and his words died.

"I was with Aiden," Joanna said, moving closer to him. She needed Zach to know she wasn't backing down.

Zach's brows furrowed. "How long have you two been sneaking around?"

Aiden answered quickly. "There wouldn't have been

any sneaking if you hadn't given both of us a hard time about seeing each other."

Zach took a step forward. "She's my sister, and I might not be the best at emotional support, but I care about her. And I know enough to see that this" –he moved his finger back and forth between them— "has to end when she goes home."

"Why is that?" Aiden crossed his arms and furrowed his brow. "Because it doesn't have to."

Zach huffed. "So are you going to move to Phoenix, or is she going to move to Freedom?"

Joanna opened her mouth to answer, but Aiden beat her to it.

"I'll move if that's the option we decide on, but it isn't your decision to make. It's between Joanna and me."

When the meaning of Aiden's words settled in her racing mind, she couldn't have spoken a word if her life depended on it. It felt as if all of the air had been sucked from her lungs, and she couldn't look away from Aiden. His determination was captivating. Did he mean it?

Before she'd gathered the nerve to speak, he continued, "This isn't a fling. I love her, and we're going to make it work. It would be great if you could get on board."

Zach eyed Joanna, but she couldn't think of anything to add, so she nodded her head in agreement. Aiden had adequately defended their relationship, and pride bloomed in her chest.

With a shake of his head, Zach said, "There isn't any snow in Phoenix, my friend. Good luck with that."

"I don't need snow. I need Joanna."

With a step back, Zach turned his attention to Joanna. "I don't want you to get hurt."

"No one has to get hurt." She reached for her brother, but he took another step back, just out of her reach, before turning on his heels and heading for the stairs without a backward glance.

Joanna released the strained breath she'd been holding. "Maybe he just needs some time."

Aiden rubbed a hand up and down her arm. "I hope so. I think he'll come around."

She turned to him and wrapped her arms around his middle. "I wouldn't ask you to move," she whispered against his chest.

"But I would."

"Don't make any big decisions yet. We have a lot to think about." She had more to think about than he knew. She'd applied for the marketing position at the resort last week, but she was terrified to get his hopes up in case she didn't get a call back.

She pushed up onto her toes and kissed him soundly, trying her best to force the worry from his eyes. "Don't worry about him. I love you, and we're going to work this out."

She didn't doubt that things would work out for the best. Her prayers had been filled with her life decisions lately, and her heart wasn't as heavy as it had once been.

"I love you too." Aiden kissed her head and didn't release his grip on her hand until it slipped from her grasp like a slipknot, pulled from both ends in separate directions.

## 24

*A*iden nervously tapped his heel in the quiet church. How had everything gotten so mixed up? He wanted to reach for Joanna's hand, but her brother sitting beside her might not like that. It was probably best not to provoke him.

He hadn't gotten a chance to talk things out with Zach since he found out about the relationship. Judging from his silence, Zach still wasn't happy about it. Aiden's other friend, Derek, sat at the end of the pew, ignoring the tension hanging in the air.

The Christmas Eve candlelight service began, and Aiden focused his attention on the altar. How long had it been since he'd gotten on his knees at God's feet? He snuck a glance at Joanna and Zach. Maybe it had been too long.

Did he owe Zach an apology? The peacekeeping part of Aiden's heart said yes. He hadn't been honest with his friend when it came to something important—Joanna.

What was left of his heart told him that his relationship with Joanna wasn't something he needed to apologize for. They hadn't done anything wrong. He turned his attention to her. The dim lights in the sanctuary cast shadows on her face, but he already knew every line and curve of her profile. He didn't need to look at her to know that she was the one God had sent to him.

No, it wasn't wrong. It was right if it had led him back to the Lord. He needed her in his life. He felt a blanket of peace rest on his shoulders as he acknowledged his commitment to her.

Stick candles skirted with paper cups were passed down the aisles. Joanna handed them to him one by one, and he passed each to his mother beside him until everyone on the pew held one.

Aiden listened as the story of Christ's birth was recounted from the book of Luke: the Light of the world, come to save us from our sins.

His heart was heavy as he gripped the thin base of the candle to steady its shaking. His sin felt heavy. His selfishness felt like a blot on his life since his dad's death, and he knew he was ready to live for someone else and something bigger than himself.

Bowing his head, he prayed. *Father, I'm sorry. I want to come home to You. I've been trying to do things my way, but it hasn't worked.*

With his eyes closed, he felt the warmth of Joanna's hand encircle his. The Lord commands his followers to cast their worry aside in the book of Matthew. Aiden's new focus would be to give his troubles to the Lord and pray for the wisdom to do what was right.

The service ended, and the lights brightened as

everyone made their way to the exit. They stopped to catch up with neighbors and friends, as well as welcome visitors alike.

After they'd dropped their extinguished candles in a basket in the vestibule, Zach stretched his arms above his head and said, "I'll meet you at the car. I have to find the restroom."

"On your right around that corner," Aiden offered.

Zach stepped into the crowd without a word.

Aiden laid a hand on his mother's arm. "We'll be there soon. Zach can follow me."

Derek stepped up beside Aiden's mother. "I'll head on over now and help out in the kitchen."

His mother smiled. "You're the sweetest." She patted Joanna's arm as she passed. "See you at the house. Be safe."

Aiden pulled Joanna to stand with him beside the wall and out of the way of the people filing out the door. "What did you think of the candlelight service?"

Joanna tucked her blonde hair behind an ear and said, "It was beautiful. I'm glad Mom and Dad are getting to spend Christmas with my brother and his family, but this is the first year I won't get to sit around my parents' living room while Dad reads us the story of Jesus's birth." She shrugged. "I'm thankful I got to worship with you tonight... with at least a part of both of our families."

Aiden wrapped an arm around her shoulders and pulled her close, kissing the top of her head. "Thank you for pointing me in the right direction. I wouldn't be here tonight without you."

"It wasn't all me. I planted the seed, but you took the steps."

He looked around, trying to determine how much time he might have with her before Zach returned. "I think God sent you to me. Because I needed to fix my relationship with Him. Is that crazy?"

Joanna rested her chin on his chest and looked up at him. "It's not crazy at all. God leads us to places and people we don't always understand."

Aiden laid a hand on her head and held her close. "I love you."

He spotted Zach rounding the corner and released her slowly. "Are you going to ride with him?" Aiden jerked his chin toward her brother.

She shook her head. "No, he hasn't spoken to me since we told him about us. I don't feel like being silently reprimanded the whole ride."

Zach found his way to them, and they all made their way to the parking lot.

Aiden typed into the messenger app on his phone. "You can follow me to Mom's, but I just sent you the address in case we get separated."

With only a nod, Zach climbed into his car. If he was upset that Joanna had jumped into Aiden's truck, he didn't show it.

Aiden pushed the concern for his friend's disdain from his mind. It was Christmas Eve, and he was determined to make the most of the time he had left with his girlfriend and his friend.

## 25

*A*iden was quiet as they drove to his mom's house. She knew he was worried about the rift with her brother, but she was confident that the three of them would work everything out. Zach would have to come to terms with her new relationship. Wouldn't he?

When they pulled into the drive of a smaller cottage-style house nestled in the pine trees, she stopped Aiden with her hand on his arm before he got out of the truck.

"Listen, Zach will come around. I think he's trying to look out for both of us, but it's hard for him to accept that he might be wrong and that this could work out between us. He just needs some time."

Aiden nodded and laid a comforting hand on the back of her head. He kissed her forehead and whispered, "I know. This trip hasn't been what he expected since his injury."

Joanna huffed. "Tell me about it. Life hasn't been fair, and I've had to hear all about it."

He smiled and released her. "Let's have fun tonight."

Zach met them at Aiden's truck and walked to the door behind them. He opened the front door and gestured for Joanna and Zach to enter first.

Joanna tugged at her scarf as the warmth of the cottage seeped through her woolen layers. Inside, it was bright and greenery touched every surface. Garland and pine hung on the mantle, over the doorways, and around a supporting beam that separated the open kitchen from the living area.

Aiden reached for Joanna's coat and scarf as his mother stepped out of the kitchen.

"Welcome, welcome." Aiden's mother extended her arms to wrap Joanna in a hug before moving to Zach. "Dinner is ready. Derek is setting the table."

"Your home is beautiful, Ms. Clark," Joanna said in wonder. "This is a gift for you." She handed over the small wrapped box.

"Please call me Jan. Thank you, dear. I'll put this with the other gifts to open after dinner." She took Zach's coat and hung it on the rack. "I've lived here since I married Aiden's father thirty years ago."

"So, this is where you grew up?" Joanna asked Aiden. "It really feels like... home."

Aiden chuckled. "To me, it is. It's not much, but Mom knows how to make a house a home."

Jan placed a hand on his shoulder as she passed. "Thank you, son." She turned to her guests and smiled. "Make yourself at home. Aiden will get you something to drink."

Joanna helped Aiden with the drinks, and everyone was seated at the table within minutes.

"Jan, everything smells delicious," Zach said.

Derek rubbed his hands together. "You said it. I haven't had a meal like this since I was here for Thanksgiving."

Jan smiled, and her rounded cheeks lifted. "I hope it tastes as good as it smells. Would anyone like to return thanks?"

"I will," Aiden offered.

Jan's eyes were the same beautiful green as her son's, but they held a silver sheen as light reflected off the moisture in her eyes. She nodded.

All heads were bowed as Aiden began. "Lord, we are honored to celebrate the birth of Your Son. Thank You for Your sacrifice and our salvation. We thank You for this food as we come together with family and friends. May it nourish our body and fuel our bodies to Your service. In Jesus name we pray. Amen."

Joanna's heart was overflowing with joy as everyone filled their plates with Jan's delicious dinner. Zach seemed to relax as Jan asked him questions about the coffee shop and his snowboarding experiences with Aiden. Soon, Aiden and Derek were swapping back and forth recounting a midsummer hike when one of Derek's training dogs got scared of a squirrel and laughing their way through. Joanna found herself chuckling at their tales of antics, and then belly laughing as Zach recounted some of her ungraceful falls trying to snowboard the week before.

After dinner, everyone moved to the living room where Jan passed out gifts to each of them and kept the one Joanna had brought.

Jan stood in front of the fireplace holding the small gift in her hands. "Thank you all for being here tonight. It means so much to me to have a house full for Christmas."

Aiden stood and wrapped his mother in a hug. "Love you, Mom."

"I love you too, son," she whispered against his scruffy cheek.

Pulling away and wiping her cheeks, Jan said, "Now, let's open these presents!"

Zach ripped into the paper covering a small box no bigger than the palm of his hand. "Thank you, Jan. You didn't have to get us anything."

Jan swatted the air in front of her. "I needed someone to buy for, and any friends of Aiden's might as well be family."

Joanna rubbed her fingertips over the wrapping paper on the box she held. She loved her family, but how blessed would she be to call herself a part of this family too?

Aiden held up his unwrapped gift with a smile on his face. "Is this your way of telling me to shave?" He rubbed his two-day scruff with the other hand.

Jan tugged at the wrapping on her own gift. "You know your father always thought a clean face was a better look."

Aiden tucked the shaving kit into the chair beside him and stood to hug his mother. "I know. I have to shave at least two days a week for work. We're not allowed to have beards at the fire station." He kissed his mother's cheek. "But I can keep it up more often. The kit looks great."

Derek laughed as he pulled the Bluetooth tracking device from a small box. "I can find hikers lost in the woods, but I'm not expected to keep up with my truck keys?"

Jan grinned. "I thought you needed one less thing to track. Plus, I bet you could put it on one of the new training puppies in case he runs off."

Derek rubbed his chin. "That's a smart idea."

Jan gasped as she pulled the apron from the box. She read, "Home is where the heart is." One hand fell on her chest. "Thank you. I love it."

"Thank you for having us," Joanna said. Her gift sat unopened in her lap.

"Your turn, Jo," Zach prompted.

Tucking her fingers under the flap of gift wrap, she ripped into the paper and discarded it on the floor beside her. She opened the hard, square box to find it stuffed with tissue paper. Everyone watched in anticipation as Joanna pulled the stuffing from the box.

She bit her lip as she stared down at the contents of the box.

"What is it?" Zach asked.

Joanna's eyes tingled as she answered, "It's a snow globe." She pulled the fragile ball from the box and held it at eye level. Specks of white floated above the town at the bottom.

"It's Freedom," Jan said. "I wanted you to remember."

The unspoken end of the sentence pierced Joanna's heart.

*When you're gone.*

Forcing her breaths to come evenly, Joanna set the snow globe on the end table beside her and hugged Jan. "Thank you." Would she see Aiden's mother again before the new year when she would have to go? She wanted to brand this hug—this night—into her memory.

It was one of the good days—one of those days she would remember forever.

"I would never forget you," Joanna whispered.

Jan shook her head slightly. "Not me, sweetie."

Joanna turned to Aiden—the man who had stolen her heart. He had encouraged her, built her up, supported her, and promised to fight for the life they wanted together.

She knew in that moment that she wouldn't ask him to uproot his life here for her. He'd offered to leave everything he loved in Freedom for her.

But she wanted Freedom.

She wanted Aiden, and Jan, and Freedom.

Aiden extended his hand to Joanna, and she stepped from Jan's embrace.

Pulling her close, he whispered, "I have a present for you too."

She nodded. "I have to get yours out of Zach's car."

Zach kept his head down as he picked up a wad of gift wrap. "I'll help you clean up."

"I'll clean up the kitchen," Derek volunteered.

Jan lifted her chin toward the door. "You two go."

Joanna grabbed her coat and scarf from the rack and hurried out into the cold night. A thin layer of fluffy snow covered the ground, brightening the darkness. She'd just grabbed the small box from the car when Aiden stepped out onto the porch, a thin, square package tucked under his arm.

She met him on the porch and leaned her hip against the railing.

"Merry Christmas." Aiden handed her the gift.

She exchanged it for the one in her hand. "You first."

His gaze held hers as he unwrapped it. When the box was free of its wrapping, he looked down to open it.

"It's a wallet," Joanna explained. "Of course, you know that. But it's made out of repurposed fire hose."

Aiden rubbed his fingertips over the embossed Maltese Cross. His smile grew as he said, "That's so cool. I love it." He lifted his head. "This is really cool, actually." He wrapped his arm around her neck to pull her into a hug. "Thank you."

"Is it my turn now?" she asked.

He pulled away to lean against the porch rail, crossing his arms over his chest. "Go ahead."

She unwrapped the gift to reveal a canvas photograph of Freedom Ridge. It wasn't just any photograph. It was one she'd taken from the Liberty Grille outdoor seating area. The large canvas brought out the slate blue and silvery tones in the snow-covered mountains.

"Thank you! This is amazing. It's beautiful." She smiled up at him. "Two things I love—photos and Freedom."

Aiden took the canvas from her and placed it on a nearby rocking chair with his wallet. He threaded his hands into her hair on both sides of her face and leaned in until he was close enough that the cloud of his warm breath in the cold air touched her lips.

"I love you. Merry Christmas." He whispered the words to her half a second before sealing his lips with hers.

She didn't know what to call the spaces between seconds, but she loved him in that moment and every other that was too small to confess it with words. She wound her arms around his neck and let every heartbeat pulse hard and loud in her ears. His warm lips slid over hers—the same lips that he used when he promised to love her, fight for her, and give up the home he'd spent his entire life building.

The door behind her opened, and she jolted back, pulled from the intimate moment.

Zach stood in the doorway, framed in the bright light inside the house. He cleared his throat and jerked a thumb over his shoulder. "We need to get on the road. The snow is coming in soon."

She turned to study the dark sky and caught sight of a few stray flakes falling.

"Okay. Let me get my snow globe and say good-bye to Jan."

She slipped by her brother in the doorway and found Jan tidying up the kitchen. Derek was on his way out, and Joanna said her good-byes before she opened her arms to Aiden's mother. "Thank you for having us. I wish we could stay, but Zach doesn't like driving in the snow, especially at night."

"No, no. You two need to get on your way. I'm sure we'll see each other again soon." Jan donned a knowing smile as she released Joanna. "I'm glad you came."

"Me too." Joanna picked up the snow globe and joined Aiden back on the porch. His back was leaning against the railing, and she looked around for Zach.

Aiden rose to his full height to meet her. "He's waiting for you in the car."

"He can wait a little longer." She could just make out

Aiden's smile in the dim lights shining through the windows, but it made her stomach flip. Grabbing his collar, she pulled him in and sealed her lips with his.

His shoulders relaxed, and his arms encircled her in their warmth. She felt the tension leave his body and dissolve into the cold mountain air.

The car engine roared to life, and the headlights lit up the night.

Joanna shot a frown her brother's way she hoped he could see. "I guess that's my cue."

Aiden rested his forehead against hers before dipping down to surprise her with another kiss. "Merry Christmas."

She wanted to stay. Everything about her life was torn between two options. Stay or go seemed to be the loudest these days.

Aiden jerked his chin toward the waiting car. "Go. I'll call you in a little bit to make sure you made it in safely."

The snow was falling faster now, and she reluctantly stepped away from him. On her way to the car, she smiled knowing Aiden would probably go inside to dance with his mother before heading home for the night.

Her happy thoughts were dampened as she closed the car door and found herself trapped in the silence that awaited her.

Zach shifted into reverse, but the car didn't move. "Jo, you know I care about you. I'm just trying to look out for you."

She turned to him, and she didn't recognize the man beside her. When had her brother grown up? It seemed like yesterday he was chasing her in their parents' yard.

They'd grown up, and they'd grown apart. But they were still family, and family looked out for each other. "I know. But you don't have to look out for me." She smiled, knowing everything would work out as it was meant to. "I love you, but I just need you to trust me."

Zach craned his neck to look over his shoulder and backed the car out of the driveway and into the snowy night.

## 26

The last few days had been lonely, save for a few phone calls with Aiden and a video call on Christmas morning with her family in Texas. Zach had sat beside her, commenting on little Landon's new toys at the appropriate times, but otherwise, he was closed off. She sensed he'd said his piece in the car on the way back to the resort on Christmas Eve, and neither of them were ready to reopen the wound.

Joanna adjusted her scarf around her neck and scanned the lounge. It was early, but guests filled the common room. Many stood in line at Mountain Mugs for a morning pick-me-up.

She hadn't told Zach where she was going. It wasn't the first time she'd kept her intentions from him this month, but she found herself wishing she could talk to him. Aiden's shift was almost over at the fire station, and he'd asked her to meet him here. In truth, she didn't know what Aiden had planned for the day. He'd claimed it was a surprise, but the excitement in his voice had amplified her curiosity.

She pulled her cell phone from the pocket of her coat and checked the time. Aiden wasn't expected to arrive for another ten minutes. Maybe she had time to grab them both a cup of coffee. Shoving her phone back into her pocket, she set her sights on the line at Mountain Mugs.

A strong hand gripped her upper arm, and she gasped, whirling to face Keith.

"What are you doing?" She didn't bother with pleasantries. Her brows lowered in her immediate anger.

Keith jerked her arm, sending her falling toward him. She caught herself with her other hand against his chest, and felt a jab in her stomach.

Righting herself, she looked down to see a gun wedged between them—the dangerous end of a pistol touching her middle.

She stared at the weapon and breathed. Her mind emptied as she tried to register the enormity of what lay between them. Everything could change in an instant.

"What are you doing?" she whispered. They were hidden by the stairs, but surely Keith wasn't capable of pulling the trigger in such a public place. Why would he even want to hurt her?

"Just move." He punctuated each word, and they held none of the emotion she'd come to expect from him.

The man calling the shots before her wasn't the man who had urged her to have dinner with him. He wasn't the goofy attorney she'd worked with for years. This was a man capable of using deadly force to get what he wanted.

Her pulse throbbed in her ears as she tried to think. She wasn't supposed to let anyone force her to another location. That was self-defense rule number one.

She forced a shaky breath into her lungs. This situation was different. She'd almost expected Keith might try something drastic. She just hadn't expected his threats to be so potentially fatal.

"Don't do this. Keith, please." She tried to make her words even, hanging her hopes on any shred of humanity he had left.

"I said move." His words were clipped and sure as he nudged her with the weapon.

She slowly turned her back to him, and he kept the gun leveled at her middle. Facing the lounge, she silently begged anyone to notice her. If one person gave her a second look, she could signal them with her eyes or an expression. She might even be able to move her lips to form the word help.

But no one looked at her. Not one guest glanced her way as Keith nudged her toward the elevator. Her heart sank even further. She wouldn't even be walking past the check-in desk. Wouldn't anyone look at her?

She had one final hope, and it was the only thing that told her it would be okay, even if he took her away from the lodge. Her chest rose and fell rapidly as she forced her lungs to do their job. Her hands were shaking, but at least he hadn't tied them. At least, he hadn't yet. She could still reach her phone. She could feel the outline of the rectangular device in the pocket of her coat.

He stopped her in front of the elevator, but a heavy hand weighed on her shoulder.

"Keith, can we talk about this? Please, just tell me what you want."

A rumble bubbled from Keith's chest. "I've been trying to talk to you for months now, and you've brushed me off every time. I'm tired of waiting for you to give me the time of day. I'm taking it."

The elevator doors opened, and panic gripped her chest. "Keith, wait. We can talk. Let's have a cup of coffee." The words tumbled out of her mouth like a waterfall, fast and free. If she could stall long enough, she could give Aiden time to get here.

Keith's grip tightened on her shoulder as he led her into the elevator, ignoring her pleas. She stumbled through the doorway, but he righted her by shifting his grip from her shoulder to her upper arm.

"Keith, you're hurting me." His fingers were digging into the sensitive skin on the underside of her arm. The elevator doors closed, separating her from the guests soaking up the last bit of Christmas cheer.

A whimper broke free from her throat, and she squeezed her eyes shut, pushing a tear down her cheek.

Aiden would look for her. He would know something was wrong as soon as he arrived and didn't find her waiting. He would go to Heath, and they would find her. Now, she wished she'd told Aiden about the plan she'd formed with the security guard. She hadn't wanted to worry him at the time, but in the midst of her abduction, it seemed imperative that he knew how to find her.

When the elevator doors opened to the parking garage, Keith shoved the gun into her back, urging her to move. He directed her to a dark-blue SUV and only released her shoulder to open the passenger door for her.

"Don't even think about running." His warning was sharp before he closed the door, leaving her alone in the car.

Instead of running, she scrambled for the phone in her pocket. She had the messaging app opened within seconds. One word. She only needed to send one word.

The driver's side door opened just as she hit send on a text to Aiden. She sucked in a breath when Keith lunged over the console to grab the phone from her hands.

"Stop it!" He threw the phone into the back seat and pointed the gun at her.

Every muscle in her body tightened. Her lifeline was inches away, but she couldn't risk reaching for it with the gaping hole of a pistol staring back at her. The dam holding back her fear broke, releasing a string of sobs that shook her shoulders. "Please. Don't do this." Her vision was blurry from the tears, but she could see the hardened expression on Keith's face. He wasn't letting her walk away now.

"I don't want to hurt you. Just stop crying. Everything will be okay." He said the words as if he believed them, but were they true for her?

She didn't speak as he drove out of the parking garage and away from the resort. She scanned the roads for any sign of Aiden's truck, but she didn't see it. Was he running late? Would he get her text in time?

Joanna wiped her cheeks and cast a terrified glance at Keith. How much time did she even have?

## 27

*A*iden parked in the employee lot at the resort and killed the engine. The view from the ridge was beautiful. He'd been hoping for a clear sky today. He wanted to take Joanna to his favorite spot at the lake so she could take photos.

He grabbed his beanie and hopped out of the truck. The thud of his truck door slamming pierced the peaceful mountain air, and he adjusted the covering on his head. Joanna would love the lake, but he wanted to tell her about all the good times he'd had there with his family. He'd inherited his sense of adventure from his dad, and the legacy lived on in him. The lake had been the perfect place to camp and observe the wildlife.

He made his way toward the lodge with a skip in his step he could only credit to Joanna. He had a few days left with her, and he was determined to make the best of them. Although, something had changed between them on Christmas Eve. Her departure wasn't looming over them anymore. They were both comfortable with the status of their relationship, and he rested easy knowing they would find a way to be together.

Stepping inside the lounge, the heat hit him like a security blanket. He enjoyed working at the resort. He had friends here, he liked his coworkers, and he loved the camaraderie they shared. It was nice knowing he could call on any of his friends here and they wouldn't hesitate to drop what they were doing to help him. He'd do the same for any of them. Kevin and Heath had made it their mission to look out for Joanna just as much as he had, and he appreciated their help.

Voices overlapped in the bustling lounge as he caught pieces of conversations. He scanned the room for Joanna's blonde hair, but the sunny color didn't catch his eye anywhere. Moving to a different part of the room, he parted his way through the crowd to get a better vantage point. He spotted the stairs and decided to use them to his advantage. On the fifth step, he gripped the railing and looked out over the sea of people. Families gathered and friends chatted, but he didn't see Joanna anywhere.

He spotted Zach exiting Liberty Grille, and Aiden made his way across the room. Zach hadn't looked up from his phone, so Aiden caught his arm to get his attention.

"Hey, have you seen Joanna?"

Zach's expression morphed from blank to a sneer. "Nice to see you too."

Aiden sighed. "Sorry, I'm supposed to be meeting her here, but I can't find her."

Zach shook his head. "I haven't seen her today. Let's hit the slopes. I only have a few days left."

Aiden barely heard his friend as his focus scanned the room. "I want to, but I'm really worried about Joanna."

"Dude, she probably went shopping or something." Zach's irritation was mounting.

Aiden halted his search and grabbed his friend's arm. "Did she say anything to you about Keith? He's been following her."

Zach huffed. "That guy is harmless. He was just desperate for a date."

Aiden's fingers tightened around Zach's arm. "I don't know if he's harmless or not, but Joanna has been looking over her shoulder for weeks. Didn't you notice? She's been a nervous wreck, and you didn't give her a second thought when she tried to talk to you about it."

A deep crease formed between Zach's brows. "Don't you think you're being a little extreme?"

"If Joanna was worried about him, then I am too." Aiden looked around one more time, and dread settled in his stomach. He could be overreacting, but he'd rather be safe than sorry. When he didn't catch sight of her in the crowd again, he pulled his phone from his pocket. A text from her lit up the screen.

Joanna: Heath

"She texted me six minutes ago." Aiden turned the phone around to show Zach.

Aiden dialed her number. Zach crossed his arms and waited as the rings echoed in Aiden's ear.

"Hi. You've reached—"

Disconnecting the call, Aiden jerked his chin toward the back of the lounge. "Let's go."

"Where? Stop walking so fast. My ankle is still sore."

They rounded a corner behind the Liberty Grille into a hallway of offices, banquet rooms, and conference rooms. Aiden didn't slow his pace until they reached the door marked Security.

Without knocking, Aiden entered. "Heath, have you seen Joanna today?"

The large man jerked his head up. "Not today."

Aiden rubbed his forehead. *Think. Where would she be?* "She was supposed to meet me here this morning, but I can't find her, and she isn't answering her phone."

Heath clicked on a keyboard in front of a line of monitors. "I'll check the footage. When were you supposed to meet?"

"Ten minutes ago."

Heath clicked rapidly and his attention skipped from screen to screen. "There she is."

Aiden leaned in to see, and Zach was right beside him.

Sure enough, Joanna was wearing a heavy sweater and a thick scarf. It was the style Aiden had come to expect from her this past month. Her blonde hair was pulled back into a low ponytail that draped over one shoulder.

His heartbeat thudded in his ears as the three of them watched the screen in silence. Heath sped up the video, but she stayed in the same place. She must have been waiting for him because she kept watching the entrance.

"Wait, there." Aiden pointed to the screen as a man—Keith—stepped up behind her.

"What's he doing?" Heath asked as he narrowed his eyes at the screen.

"She's walking away with him!" Aiden couldn't believe his eyes. "What is she doing?"

Zach straightened. "Maybe she took him up on that date offer."

Aiden's gaze scanned the screen for any clues. The footage was grainy, but he could see Joanna standing close to Keith as they made their way to the elevator. The time stamp reflected the time as fifteen minutes ago.

"She didn't go with him willingly." Aiden righted himself and turned to Heath who was already tapping on his phone.

"Looks like she did, bro."

Aiden was fed up with Zach's attitude, and the dam inside of him burst. "You have no idea what she's been through these last few weeks. She wouldn't have gone with him. I know it." Pointing in the general direction of the lounge, Aiden's voice rose. "She was afraid he would do something, and I know that's what's happening right now. We have to find her."

Heath held up a finger. "Here. She's headed down the mountain, away from the resort."

Aiden leaned over the security guard. "What? How do you know that?"

"She asked me to put a tracker on her phone. She didn't trust Keith, and she knew the two of you might not always be around."

Aiden's throat felt as if it dropped into his stomach. She'd feared for her safety enough that she'd wanted to be tracked? His worry jumped to a new and unwelcome level. Turning to his friend, he saw the color drain from Zach's face. "We have to go."

Heath had another phone to his ear as he watched her location on his cell. "This is Officer Mitchell—"

Zach grabbed Aiden's arm. "I can't go with you. I'm too slow." Zach pulled his phone from his pocket. "Stay on the phone with us, and we'll tell you where to go."

Aiden looked to Heath as he hung up the call. "Can you use that to track me too?" Aiden pointed to the phone Heath held.

"Give me your phone. This is elementary. It's just a tracking app."

Aiden flexed and released his fists at his sides. "So, it's connected to her phone? What if she's not with her phone?"

Heath handed Aiden's phone back. "We have to hope she is."

Aiden's nostrils flared as he tried to keep his breathing even. He didn't want to think about the alternative. "Tell me where to go. I'll keep you on my Bluetooth." He turned to leave, but Zach's hand fell on his shoulder.

"Hey, be careful, and get her back. She means everything to me."

The pain in Zach's voice was scratchy, but Aiden recognized his own fears in his friend's eyes. "She means everything to me too. I'm not coming back without her."

With that, he pushed the door open hard enough that it banged against the wall. He needed every second he could get, and time wasn't on his side.

---

## 28

*J*oanna tried to take notice of everything they passed as Keith drove. He hadn't blindfolded her or restrained her in any way, but she was terrified to make a run for it. She needed to be smart about it, and bolting without a plan would only get her lost and alone. Without her phone to call for help, she would be left wandering in the woods.

So far, she'd recognized some of the landmarks. They had to be close to Aiden's house because Keith had taken some of the same turns, and she could see the lake through the trees on their left. They were on the same side of the lake that Aiden lived on, but there had been too many changes in direction now, and she was growing confused.

The words of a hurried prayer flashed through her mind. *Lord, please give me focus. Please help me remember. Please show me how to get out of this.*

A shaky breath rattled her shoulders. *Please help Aiden and Heath find me.* They might not even know she was missing. Her heart pounded as they took another turn. It was too much. She couldn't remember all the turns, and Keith continued driving away from anything she found familiar. Panic had her hands shaking in her lap.

Aiden would find her. She knew it. Heath had everything he needed to track her, and they would do everything they could to get to her. She trusted them.

Keith jerked the SUV into a short drive that slanted down a hill. A cabin similar to Aiden's sat hidden beneath the snowy pines to the right.

"Don't move. I'll come get you." Keith opened his door and stepped out, closing it behind him.

Her mind whirled with indecision. Make a run for it? Wait for a better time? The urge to bound out of the vehicle was unbearable.

Before she had a chance to decide, Keith opened the door to the backseat and grabbed her phone from the floorboard. Her heart sank into the seat before she remembered that she didn't need to access the phone. As long as he kept it near them, it would be traceable.

She closed her eyes and drew in a deep breath. *Please, Lord, help me be patient.* She needed to wait for Aiden and Heath despite the urges to make a drastic getaway that could get her lost or shot by the madman holding her hostage.

Keith opened her door and extended his open hand to her. The last thing she wanted to do was take it, but an idea flickered into existence. Maybe if she cooperated, he would let down his guard.

She placed her hand in his and fought the urge to

shudder. His palm was clammy and cold—a sign that he wasn't as collected as he seemed.

Keith gripped her hand, and she gasped. His offered hand hadn't been a pleasantry. It was a way to restrain her. He pulled her ungracefully behind him, and she struggled to keep up with his wide stride and quick pace.

At the door, he slapped her hand against the exterior of the house and barked, "Put the other hand beside it."

With both of her hands flat against the wall beside the door, Keith retrieved a key from his coat pocket and unlocked the door. He cast a glance over his shoulder and through the wooded area surrounding the cabin before clamping his hand on her shoulder and forcing her inside.

She stood in the entryway and studied the cabin. It was laid out much like Aiden's house, but the decor was overdone. A rental property? She looked for any sign of a second exit and noted only the door leading to the porch. If the porch wrapped around the house the way Aiden's did, she could escape through that door and run around either side of the cabin.

A high zipping noise sounded behind her and she turned to find Keith pulling the tie out of the collar of his hoodie. The thin black string snapped in his hands as he approached her.

"Keith, listen." Joanna held up her hands as if she were warding off a wild animal. "I'm not going to run." In truth, she wasn't sure if she had any intentions of running or not. She wanted to be smart about the movements she made, but right now, she didn't know what to do.

He grabbed her wrists, spun her to face away from him, and forced her hands together. As he wrapped the string around them, she focused on her hands and tried to create an unnoticeable amount of space between them so she could stretch the binding enough to break free.

Keith snapped her wrists painfully close and retied them. His breath was hot in her ear, and she wanted to hide her neck from him. She was too vulnerable to him like this, and she lifted her shoulder to shrink away from him.

"I'm not going to hurt you. I just want a chance to talk."

His words should have eased her fears, but she didn't trust them. She focused on calming her rapidly beating heart and spoke with a soft voice. "We could have talked at the resort."

He stepped away from her, and she relaxed a fraction. Her tension seemed to be tied to his proximity. She'd been a ball of nerves whenever Keith was around for weeks.

She slowly turned to face him. He brushed a hand through his hair and sat ungracefully in the nearby recliner. "You wouldn't give me a chance. I don't know why you made this so difficult."

Joanna tried to look at him and see a man she'd worked with for years instead of the man who had abducted her. She hadn't known him at all when they'd worked together.

Did she really know anyone? Her brother had turned against her, and a seemingly harmless coworker had now tied her up in a remote cabin.

She could admit that she'd had a hand in pushing Zach away, but Keith's actions were unjustified. She had a right to decline every offer he'd made to take her to dinner, and she stood by that decision.

Right now, she needed to be patient and let him have his say as long as possible to give Aiden a chance to find her. She felt as if she were on display as she stood alone in front of Keith. She kept silent and prayed he would take his time talking instead of moving to anything else. She couldn't think of the alternatives he might attempt while she was tied this way.

"Don't you think we would make a great couple? I mean, we work together, we're both highly intelligent," Keith ticked off the two points on his fingers. "We could be a power couple in the office, and we would be happy in our personal lives. I know we could be great together if you would just stop and think about it."

His plea was emotional, but the desperation in his speech made it rushed. It was almost as if he were convincing himself, but she saw the moment when his mood shifted. The soft eyes narrowed, and he sat up straighter.

"You'll see. We just need to spend some time together... in a romantic cabin." He lifted his hands to indicate the perfect setting he'd created. "You'll see that we're made for each other."

She was pretty sure God hadn't created her to be forced into a relationship with an abductor against her will, but she kept silent on that point. The more Keith spoke, the hotter her panic grew within her. Where was Aiden? He should have begun looking for her only minutes after she left with Keith.

What if he wasn't coming? What if he hadn't gotten

her message or misunderstood it? Her nostrils flared as she breathed hotter and faster.

He had to be coming for her. If he wasn't, then she needed to do something. Indecision gripped her. Be patient and wait for help to arrive or act now?

Keith sighed and stood. He left her standing alone in front of the fireplace, and fear overrode every other instinct.

She watched him amble to the kitchen with his back to her. Now was her chance.

She ran. Hands tied behind her back, she maneuvered around a couch and shoved a chair at the breakfast table out of her way with a hip as she ran for the door leading to the porch.

Keith yelled behind her, but she didn't hesitate. When she reached the door, she turned her back to it and spread her tied hands as far as she could. She craned her neck to see the knob over her shoulder as she fumbled the lock.

His footsteps thundered toward her, and she screamed as he grabbed her shoulders, throwing her to the floor away from the door.

She landed on her back, crushing her hands behind her. A blinding pain shot up her arm, and she gasped. Air rushed into her lungs, but it hung there, unable to finish the motion of pushing back out. Pain like fire throbbed in the arm until it hit a threshold, falling numb beneath the weight of her body.

Keith descended on her and backhanded her left cheek. She barely felt it, overcome by the pain in her arm that had fallen back over her like a wave.

"Don't run!" Keith yelled merely inches from her face.

The words were distorted. She could only process the unbearable pain.

Keith grabbed her upper arm and jerked up, trying to pull her to her feet.

When the pain registered, it filled her lungs, and she screamed.

## 29

*A*iden gripped the steering wheel as he drove over the quiet roads outlining the lake. "How close am I?"

Heath's voice was muffled through the speakers of the truck. "Slow down. I think it's the next drive on the left. Officer Harrison, I'll let you know when you're close."

Heath had conferenced in his friend, Max Harrison, at the Martin County Police Department, and they were sending officers right behind Aiden.

"Aiden, you're right on it."

"There's a cabin here with a dark-blue SUV parked outside." Aiden whipped the truck into the drive behind the SUV. Disconnecting his phone from Bluetooth, he jumped out of the truck. "I'm keeping you on the line, but I'm putting the phone in my pocket."

"Don't engage, Aiden. Wait for the police."

"Heath, I can't wait if she's in there." Aiden wouldn't give Keith an extra minute to hurt Joanna if he could help it. His friend's words faded as he stuck the phone in his coat pocket.

Careful to be silent as he ascended the stairs to the porch, Aiden moved swiftly onto the porch and to the door. A woman screamed inside the cabin, and he darted to the window, certain he had the right cabin.

He looked through the window, but didn't see any sign of Joanna. He scanned the living room and breakfast area, and movement caught his eye on the other side of the room. Keith stood, hauling Joanna to her feet as she released another blood-chilling scream.

He couldn't wait for the police to arrive. Surely, they would be here any minute. He grabbed the phone from his pocket and spoke quickly.

"Heath, this is it. Keith has her in there, and he's hurting her. I'm going in."

"Stand down!"

Aiden shoved the phone back into his pocket and looked for anything he could use to break in. Just out of curiosity, he checked the door. Of course, it was locked. A wooden statue of a bear sat beside the door, and he picked it up. The solid piece of wood was as long as his shin and weighed enough to damage the window.

He hefted the carving at the nearest window. It broke, sending glass flying and a high-pitched shattering sound echoing through the mountains around the cabin.

Without checking to see if Keith was coming, Aiden used the side of his fist to knock out enough of the window to climb in.

Keith was backing up toward the far wall, and Joanna lay on the floor at his feet. She was turned on her side with her arms tied behind her back. Her hair sprawled out over her shoulder, concealing her face behind its curtain.

The scream he'd just heard wailed over and over in his ears. Keith had laid his hands on her, and Aiden wouldn't let it happen again. Anger was hot in his ears as his gaze landed on Keith.

The man had the decency to back away from Aiden. His eyes widened as fear wrapped Keith in its grip.

Aiden took a step toward him, and Keith darted toward a nearby room. Aiden was faster and had anticipated the move. Stepping in front of Keith, Aiden wrapped his arms around him before throwing him to the floor. Aiden pushed Keith onto his stomach and held his wrists together behind his back.

Joanna groaned as police sirens wailed in the distance.

"Hang in there. The police are coming," Aiden said.

Keith struggled to throw Aiden from where he knelt to restrain him, but Aiden was much stronger and in a position to control the fight.

The wail of the sirens grew louder. "Don't worry. They're almost here."

Keith continued to struggle, but Aiden kept him tightly restrained on the floor.

Joanna needed his reassurances. She was writhing in pain, and his heart broke every time she sucked air in through her teeth. Hopefully, the police had brought paramedics with them. If not, he knew enough to help her until they could get to medical care. He just couldn't take his hands off Keith until the police arrived.

Heavy footsteps banged against the porch outside, and

Aiden called to them. "We're in here. You'll have to send someone through the window to unlock the door."

"Aiden?" Officer Max Harrison stepped through the window.

Aiden had met Officer Harrison on various calls over the years, and they worked well together. "She needs help. Did you bring paramedics?"

"On their way." Officer Harrison unlocked the door to allow his partner to enter.

Aiden had his sights set on Joanna as the police officers relieved him of Keith. Crouching beside her, he carefully untied her hands. She winced at every movement he made. A knot protruded from her arm that was a clear indication of a break.

"Careful. Protect your arm until the paramedics get here." He wanted to wrap her in his arms and squeeze her tight, but her injuries required he keep a distance. No matter what, he wouldn't be leaving her alone. He'd spend the rest of the day at the hospital with her.

Joanna sobbed. Her face was covered in tears, and he wiped at her cheeks.

"I'm sorry. I'm here now. I love you." He loved her so fiercely that he could barely breathe.

"I'm so glad you came." Joanna's tears began anew, and he carefully moved her arm out of the way so he could pull her head to rest on his chest. Burying his face in her hair, he whispered assurances to her while the police recited Keith's rights.

Aiden tried not to think about Joanna's wrist. The unnatural angle in her arm turned his stomach, and he often saw gruesome and horrible scenes in his line of work. It was different when someone you loved was hurt. His training faded into the recesses of his mind as his emotions took control.

Paramedics made their way into the room, and Aiden moved back just enough to let them assess her arm. Her cheek was swollen and a little red.

"Is anything else injured?" a dark-haired paramedic asked.

Joanna shook her head. "I think my cheek is just bruised. He backhanded me, but I fell with all my weight on my wrist. I couldn't catch myself."

Aiden swallowed the bile that rose in his throat. Hearing about what she'd endured caused strange physical reactions in him.

Aiden stood by her, holding her uninjured hand as they moved her to the ambulance and closed the doors. The sirens wailed through the mountains as they pulled out onto the main road, but the driver silenced them after a while unless they passed through an intersection.

Moving out of the way of the paramedic, Aiden squeezed Joanna's hand. "I'm going to call Zach and let him know where we're headed."

Joanna nodded. "Okay. Thank you."

He pressed the call button and waited half a ring before Zach answered.

"Did you find her?"

"She's okay. We found her, and the police have Keith in custody."

Zach breathed a sigh of relief.

"We're on our way to Freedom Memorial. She has a broken arm, and she's shaken up."

"I'll meet you there."

Aiden ended the call and focused his attention on Joanna. Her eyes were closed, and a pained expression covered her face.

"I'm here." He squeezed her uninjured hand. "I'm here, and I'm never letting go."

## 30

*A*iden paced alone in the waiting room at Freedom Memorial Hospital. The doctors were attending to Joanna and deciding on a course of treatment for her wrist, and the suspense was overwhelming. He knew she was okay. He'd seen it with his own eyes, but being away from her when she was hurting was difficult. Never in his life had he cared so much about the outcome of a conversation.

The nearby elevator dinged, and Officer Max Harrison stepped out. Aiden was thankful for the department's quick response, but Max's expression was anything but relieved.

Aiden halted his nervous pacing and faced the approaching officer.

Max lowered his brows and crossed his arms over his chest. "How is she?"

Aiden eyed the doors leading to her room. "I don't know. They're meeting with her now."

"You were way out of line running into a scene without waiting for backup. You knew better."

Aiden mirrored Max's stance. "I knew Joanna was in trouble, and I wasn't going to twiddle my thumbs until you showed up. I stand by my actions."

Max shook his head. "I'm just glad it worked out. Both of you could've gotten into a lot of trouble."

Joanna hadn't escaped that fate, and Aiden rubbed a hand over his lowered chin. "Yeah, I know. I heard her scream, and I was seeing red." He looked up at the officer. "I didn't have a choice."

Max's heavy hand landed on Aiden's shoulder. "She's lucky we found her so soon."

The elevator dinged, and Zach appeared in the hallway looking right and left frantically until he spotted Aiden. Zach rushed over. "Is she okay?"

Aiden pointed to the nearby doors. "They're working on a plan. She might need surgery."

Zach nodded and looked at the floor. "I hate that. This shouldn't have happened. What about that Keith guy?"

Max extended his hand. "Officer Harrison. Keith Sanders has been taken into custody."

Zach gripped the offered hand. "Thanks, I'm Zach Drake, Joanna's brother."

"It's a pleasure to meet you."

"Likewise. Thank you for your service. I appreciate you helping my sister."

"Anytime." Max looked at his watch. "I need to head out. I'll catch you later."

They said their good-byes, and Aiden and Zach didn't

speak once the officer was gone. Zach rubbed the back of his neck and studied the floor. "I guess I owe you a big apology."

Aiden sat in a nearby chair and gestured for Zach to take a seat. "I don't know how things got so complicated, but I never had anything but good intentions with Joanna."

"I know that now." Zach propped his elbows on his knees. "This past month hasn't been anything like I thought it would be."

Aiden chuckled. "I know what you mean. It's been life changing for me too. If you'd have told me a month ago I'd have kept secrets from my best friend and fallen in love with his sister, I'd have called you crazy."

Zach turned to Aiden. "You love her?"

Aiden nodded. "I do. I'd do anything for her. She's not like anyone I've ever met before. She kind of set me straight from the beginning, and I think that was what I needed. You know, someone to tell me to get my act together. Then everything else just kind of fell into place. I didn't want to tell you because I knew you'd freak out. But on the other hand, I couldn't walk away from her, and I wanted to tell you."

Zach sighed. "I've been so worried about myself and the injury that I didn't care about anyone else. I should have listened to you both. I thought I was protecting her, but it looks like you did a pretty good job of that on your own." He flashed a genuine grin at his observation.

"I would never let anything happen to her. If it's within my power to help, I'd be there in a heartbeat."

"Like you were today," Zach pointed out. "I get it. I also know you're a good guy, and that should have been enough for my sister. You've always been friendly and good to people. I should have thought more about the good man that you are instead of all the ways I thought it couldn't work out for the two of you."

Aiden tapped his heel on the bland tiled floor. "I appreciate that. I don't know what comes next for us or where this will end up, but we both want it to work."

"Did you mean it when you said you would move? For her?"

Aiden took a deep breath and nodded. "Yeah. I would. I won't find snow in Phoenix, but I don't need that in my life the way I need her."

Zach stared out the window, lost in his thoughts. "I've been so blind. I'm sorry, man."

Aiden bumped his shoulder against Zach's. "It all worked out."

"Not all of it." Zach seemed very interested in a black speck that marred the white floor. "I saw Stacy right before I came out here."

It took Aiden a moment to place the name in his mind, but he eventually recalled their freshman year at college. "You mean the Stacy that you broke up with right before college?"

"To be fair, she broke up with me."

That made more sense. Zach had moped the entire first semester of college over Stacy. "What happened?"

Zach shrugged. "Everything was the same. I still love her. Except now I live in Arizona, and she lives in Wyoming."

"I can't tell you what's right for you and Stacy. Every relationship is different."

"Yeah. I know. I've just been stuck in my own head a lot lately, and I wasn't the best friend or brother. It's no excuse, but for what it's worth, I'm sorry I was a jerk."

"Water under the bridge."

"I really hope things work out for you and Jo."

"Me too. If things go my way, we might be brothers one day."

Zach jerked back. "Dude, you're not asking her to marry you, are you?"

Aiden laughed at Zach's reaction. "Not today, but she's the one for me."

Zach's eyes widened. "Wow. Didn't see that one coming."

A woman in a white coat stepped into the waiting room. "Are you the family of Ms. Drake?"

Aiden and Zach stood to greet her.

Zach answered for both of them. "Yes. Do you have any news?"

"I'm Doctor Tate. I'll be performing surgery on her fractured radius. We'll begin shortly, and the surgery should last about an hour. After that, she'll be in recovery for another hour, and we'll decide from there when she's ready for visitors."

Aiden extended his hand to the doctor. "Thank you. We'll be here if you have any other news."

Doctor Tate shook hands with Aiden and then Zach before she left with a promise to let them know the outcome of the surgery.

Aiden fell back into the rigid waiting room chair. "Looks like we have a long wait ahead of us."

Zach grabbed the remote to the small television mounted in the corner of the waiting room. "ESPN?"

"Please." Anything to distract Aiden from the hours of worry that lay ahead of him.

## 31

*J*oanna opened her eyes and quickly snapped them shut. The lights were too bright.

Trying again, she opened her eyes a mere centimeter and judged that the light wasn't as bright as she'd previously thought. They drifted closed again, and she waited before opening them once more. Fuzziness filled the room, and she rolled her head on the pillow.

"There you are," a feminine voice said. "I'm almost finished here. How are you feeling?"

The woman was wearing scrubs. A nurse. Joanna didn't speak.

"We'll wait a few more minutes before I let your visitors in."

Joanna lazily opened and closed her eyes as her vision cleared. Slowly, she regained her senses.

The nurse was standing in front of a computer on a wheeled cart nearby. When she noticed Joanna was more awake, she asked again, "How are you feeling?"

"Fine." Her throat was raw like she'd swallowed sand or knives. "My throat."

"That will get better. They had to intubate you for the surgery. It went well, and your visitors can come in soon."

"Who?"

The young nurse's eyes widened. "The two men in the waiting room."

"Oh, thank you." Zach and Aiden had stayed. Had Zach told their parents? She didn't want them to worry.

A few minutes later, the nurse slipped out with a promise to return soon. When the door opened, it was Aiden and Zach who appeared.

"Hey, sis. You feeling okay?" One of Zach's eyes squinted as if he were bracing for her to hit him.

"I'm okay. Just groggy. The nurse said the surgery went well."

Aiden smiled, and her focus shifted to his joy. How much worse off would she be if he hadn't showed up when he did?

He moved to the other side of her bed and picked up her hand. "The doctor filled us in. I'm glad it's over though."

The feel of his warm skin was like the sun on a beautiful morning, dragging her from the remnants of sleep. "Me too."

Zach moved a step closer to her bed. "I called Mom and Dad to let them know. They were shook up, but I told them you were okay."

"Thank you. I'll call them later." Her arm was heavy, but she didn't want to look at it yet. The pressure she felt was a reminder of the pain.

Zach looked around the small hospital room and stuttered, "Well, I'll let you two have a minute. I'm going to the cafeteria. Either of you want anything?"

They both shook their heads and waited until the door closed behind Zach to look at each other.

"You scared me," Aiden said.

The worry in his eyes had her tugging him closer by the hand she held.

Aiden cleared his throat and sat on the bed beside her. "I don't think I've ever been that scared in my life. If I'd been later, or—"

Joanna cut him off. "Thank you. For coming for me. You saved me. There's no sense in playing out the what-ifs." She traced a lazy finger over his jawline. "Everything is okay."

He grabbed her uninjured wrist and pressed her knuckles to his lips. "I love you."

"I love you too."

"I can't wait until you're released."

"I have no idea when that'll be, but I don't know if I'll feel up to traveling next week."

"Stay as long as you want. Mom has a spare room you can use. I already called her and let her know what happened. I can take a few days off to drive you back to Phoenix when you're feeling up to it."

The idea of returning to work wasn't appealing with a cast up her arm. What would her coworkers at Miller and Baker think when she returned? What would they do now that Keith was incarcerated?

Everything had gotten much messier than she'd expected, and she didn't want to think about returning to work just yet. "I'm not sure about anything right now." She squeezed his hand with the small amount of energy she had. "Thank you for being here."

Aiden's smile was like a balm to the pain. "Always."

~

TWO WEEKS LATER, Joanna stared out the window of her office at Miller and Baker. The middle of the week bustle had overtaken the city, and there was movement everywhere.

She smiled and cradled her cell phone in her lap. A cast still covered one arm to the elbow, but she was getting used to the extra weight.

Excitement filled her, spreading from the inside out. She covered her smile with a hand and sucked a deep breath in through her nose.

One phone call had changed her life. It was funny how her life had crept along, every day the same for years, but now, it was changing in an instant.

One more phone call would seal the change forever, turning the direction of her life on its end. She closed her eyes and felt a joy stir in her heart unlike anything she'd experienced in a long time.

She whispered into her quiet office, "Thank You, Lord." The prayer was short, but it was one of the most heartfelt prayers she'd ever uttered.

Her hand trembled as it hovered over Aiden's name on the phone. It was the middle of a workday, and he might not answer. She tried not to get her hopes up as she pressed the button to call.

He answered on the second ring. She could hear the smile in his voice.

"Hey, Love. To what do I owe this midday call?"

She felt moisture cover her eyes and swallowed hard. "Hey. I have some news."

"I'm only accepting good news today. Lay it on me."

Oh, she had good news. "I'm quitting my job."

Aiden was silent for three weighted seconds. "What? Why? Is everything okay?"

One tear escaped, and she brushed it away. It was a happy tear. The best kind. "Everything is great. I got another job."

"Joanna?" The hesitation in Aiden's voice was thick with curiosity and a little worry.

"You're talking to the newest member of the Freedom Ridge Resort marketing team."

"What?" Aiden screamed. "You're kidding!"

Joanna laughed at his excitement. The elation inside of her needed a release. "I'm not kidding. I just got off the phone with Kevin. I start in four weeks. He's giving me time to work out a two-week notice here and get my life moved to Freedom."

Her heart felt so full it might burst. Saying the words out loud made them real. "I'm flying up tomorrow to finalize everything and sign the paperwork. I still have to book a flight, but… I was so excited, I had to tell you first."

Aiden's voice was deep and thick with emotion. "I love you so much. Come to me."

Joanna bit her bottom lip to stifle the urge to squeal like a teenager.

"I'm coming home."

# EPILOGUE

*J*oanna captured another photo of the barista at Mountain Mugs handing a latte to a customer. Casey brushed her long ponytail over her shoulder and smiled. Since starting her job at the resort, Joanna had become good friends with Casey, and when she mentioned she needed more material for the website, Casey had volunteered to model.

Checking the image on her camera screen, Joanna smiled. "I think that's a wrap. You're a natural."

Casey chuckled. "I just did my job, and you took photos. What's hard about that?"

"You smile while you work. Not many people do that."

Casey shrugged. "Sounds like they're in the wrong profession."

Joanna agreed. Since leaving Miller and Baker and moving to Freedom, she'd found a level of happiness she hadn't experienced before. "Thanks for letting me lurk around. I'm going to see if Haven will let me follow her around for a while."

Casey stepped to the register to attend to another customer and waved her good-byes.

Joanna's circle of friends had grown immensely in the last three months. She'd met all of her coworkers at the resort since taking the marketing job back in January, and they'd welcomed her into the resort family with open arms.

There were times when she missed her family in Phoenix, but she kept in touch with them every day. Her mom and dad had supported her decision to move and change jobs, and Zach had even helped her move.

The Christmas decorations were long gone, but the Rocky Mountain peaks were still blindingly white outside the windows of Liberty Grille. She moved her way around the perimeter of the restaurant until she spotted Haven sitting alone at a table.

Joanna removed her camera and stuck it into the carrying case. "Hey. I hope you haven't been waiting long."

"I just sat down." They had lunch together every Wednesday. "How's it going?"

"Great. I got some good material for the Mountain Mugs section of the site this morning, and I was hoping I could follow you around after lunch."

Haven shrugged. "Sounds good to me." A mischievous smile spread across her lips. "What are you doing after work?"

Joanna rested her elbows on the table and leaned in. "I'm having dinner with Aiden and his mom tonight. What about you?"

"We're going to Evelyn's tonight. Nothing special."

The higher pitch in Haven's voice held a secret. The

event planner was friendly, but rarely so chipper. "Okay. Well, we have dinner with Aiden's mom at least once a week. I guess that might not be anything special to some people, but I always look forward to it."

Jan had taken Joanna under her wing as soon as she moved to Freedom. Knowing Aiden's work schedule kept him away for days at a time, his mother sought to include Joanna in everything she could. They spent a lot of time together, but the company eased the ache of missing her own mother.

Haven smoothed her hands over the napkin in her lap. "You're blessed to have Jan for a mother-in-law."

Joanna chuckled. "She isn't my mother-in-law. We're not married." She desperately wanted to add a "yet" to the end of that sentence, but she also didn't want to presume. She and Aiden had talked about marriage a few times, and she knew enough to know he wanted to be married one day. She just didn't know when.

For her, she knew Aiden was the one. She would gladly spend her life with him. She was already living a blessed life. Spending the rest of it with Aiden by her side would be an answer to her prayers.

Haven bit her bottom lip, and the corners of her mouth turned up just as the waitress stepped up to their table. They both said their hellos to Ivy before she took down their orders and retreated to the kitchen.

Joanna narrowed her eyes at Haven once they were alone again. "Do you have something to tell me? You're acting weird."

Haven shook her head. "Nope." She pulled her phone from her pocket. "I have to show you Miah's school pictures. They're perfect." Haven's daughter had started pre-k this year, and the proud mother never failed to mention how well Miah was doing.

They scrolled through the posed photos with a bright background for spring, and Joanna asked for a photo to frame in her office. She'd grown close to Miah while hanging out with Haven.

Joanna's phone buzzed, and she checked the screen. A smile spread across her face as she read Aiden's text.

Aiden: I can't wait to see you tonight.

She typed out a quick reply.

Joanna: Me too. I love you.

Setting her phone down on the table, she turned her attention back to her friend. Her life and her heart were overflowing with a happiness that she hadn't known she was missing before. She closed her eyes and thanked God for sending her to Freedom and bringing her home.

JOANNA PARKED behind Aiden's truck at Jan's house fifteen minutes early. She'd insisted on driving herself since her apartment was out of his way home from his mom's. It had been over two days since she'd seen him, and she practically jumped from her car and bounded up the porch stairs.

Throwing open the door, she gave a loud, "Hello!" before shrugging her coat from her shoulders. She didn't feel like a guest in Jan's home anymore, and she hadn't knocked before entering in weeks.

Aiden rose from his stool at the kitchen bar with a

smile. Would there ever come a day when the sparkle in his eyes didn't warm her insides? Sometimes, she liked to pinch the skin on the back of her hand to remind herself she wasn't dreaming. This handsome man loved her and had run headlong into danger to save her. His mother made a homecooked meal for them every week. They attended church together, holding hands through every prayer. She worked at a ski resort in the gorgeous Rockies surrounded by her friends.

The overwhelming love of it all hit her square in the chest from time to time, and she had to remind herself to breathe. God had blessed her abundantly, and she had dedicated her life to serving Him and spreading the good news of His Kingdom.

Joanna opened her arms to Aiden, and his intense gaze didn't waver from her. His gaze traveled from her eyes to her hair where his fingers slid into it at her temples before finally settling on her lips.

"I missed you," he whispered. The reverence in his voice stopped her breath.

"I missed you too."

She wanted him to kiss her. It had been too long since they had been together, and she couldn't find it in her to care that his mother was nearby.

Instead of kissing her, he took one step back and knelt in front of her, holding one hand in his.

Her eyes widened, and she gasped. "Aiden." Her free hand flew to her mouth.

"I love you, Joanna. I didn't know I needed you so badly until you were standing in front of me. You changed my life, and I want to spend the rest of my days beside you."

"Me too. That's what I want. Yes, yes, yes!" The words spilled from her mouth, quick and sure.

"You didn't let me get to the good part."

She laughed through fresh tears as Aiden pulled a ring from his pocket. The circular solitaire sat proud atop a white gold band. "I'm sorry. Go ahead."

"I want to grow old with you and build a family with you. Will you marry me?"

Joanna nodded as a choked sound tore from her throat. "Yes." The sobs shook her body as he stood to wrap her in his arms. He held her tight until she'd exhausted the well of happy tears.

When her shoulders stopped shaking, he pulled back enough to wipe her cheeks and cradle her face in his hands. "I love you."

"I love you too."

He released a relieved breath and claimed her mouth with his. The rush of his joy filled her as he pressed her closer to his body.

This was the beginning of a new chapter in her life. The one where she and Aiden made a life of love and happiness together in Freedom.

Ready for Haven's story? Return to Freedom Ridge in *Love Pact with the Hero*, the second book in the Heroes of Freedom Ridge series.

TWO BEST FRIENDS. One little girl's prayers. And a love pact that may be the answer to all of their Christmas wishes.

~

Join in all the fun at our Facebook Reader Group
www.facebook.com/groups/freedomridgereaders
For sneak peeks, giveaways, and tons of Christmas romance fun!

# HEROES OF FREEDOM RIDGE SERIES

(Year 1)

**Rescued by the Hero (Aiden and Joanna)**

Mandi Blake

**Love Pact with the Hero (Jeremiah and Haven)**

Liwen Y. Ho

(Year 2)

**Healing the Hero (Daniel and Ashley)**

Elle E. Kay

**Stranded by the Hero (Carson and Nicole)**

Hannah Jo Abbott

(Year 3)

**Reunited with the Hero (Max and Thea)**

M.E. Weyerbacher

**Forgiven by the Hero (Derek and Megan)**

Tara Grace Ericson

# OTHER BOOKS BY MANDI BLAKE

**Blackwater Ranch Series**

Remembering the Cowboy

Charmed by the Cowboy

Mistaking the Cowboy

**Unfailing Love Series**

Complete small-town Christian romance series

Just as I Am

Never Say Goodbye

Living Hope

Beautiful Storm

All the Stars

What if I Loved You

**The Blushing Brides Series**

The Billionaire's Destined Bride

The Cowboy's Runaway Bride

**The Heroes of Freedom Ridge Series**

Multi-author series

Rescued by the Hero

## ABOUT THE AUTHOR

Mandi Blake was born and raised in Alabama where she lives with her husband and daughter, but her southern heart loves to travel. Reading has been her favorite hobby for as long as she can remember, but writing is her passion. She loves a good happily ever after in her sweet Christian romance books and loves to see her characters' relationships grow closer to God and each other.

www.mandiblakeauthor.com

## ACKNOWLEDGMENTS

I never anticipated making so many friends when I decided to write books. Before I knew it, my friends were my co-workers. Writing this book with the other amazing authors in this series has been a wonderful experience, and I've grown closer to them over the last year.

I want to thank my beta readers, Pam Humphrey, Jenna Eleam, Elizabeth Maddrey, and Tanya Smith for helping me iron out the details of this story. I also want to thank my sister, Kenda Goforth, for being my biggest supporter.

As always, I appreciate my editor, Brandi Aquino, for making this book shine. Amanda Walker created beautiful covers for every book in the Heroes of Freedom Ridge series.

I also want to thank Tara Grace Ericson for reaching out to me about this series. I had no idea that we would become best friends, but I'm blessed to have her in my life. She also deserves a big thanks for bringing together this wonderful group of authors. Hannah Jo Abbott, Elle

E. Kay, M. E. Weyerbacher, and Liwen Y. Ho were amazing to work with, and I'm glad we grew so close as we wrote this series together.

Last, but never least, I want to thank you for reading. I'm blessed to be able to write stories about the Lord and spread the word about his kingdom, and I've come to know many of my readers as friends. It means so much to me that we're able to grow closer to each other as we worship the Lord, and I'm glad you took a chance on this book. I hope to be able to give you many more stories of hope and faith in the future.

# REMEMBERING THE COWBOY

## BLACKWATER RANCH BOOK 1

**They have unfinished business. She just can't remember what it is.**

Camille Vanderbilt is headed back home to Wyoming with one goal: find her old best friend and give him a piece of her mind for ghosting her six years ago. She won't let anyone stand in her way… until a deer runs into the road and causes her to wreck and forget almost everything.

Noah Harding lives a simple life as a firefighter and rancher until Camille crashes back into his life. When a call at the fire station sends him to save his old best friend's life, he thinks he might get a second chance until her influential stepdad gives a reminder that his old threats still stand.

When Camille runs into Noah in town, she knows he's important to her, but her memories are still fuzzy.

Noah is hesitant to get close to her when it means having to sacrifice everything to be with her.

She thinks it's a new beginning, but he knows it shouldn't have ever ended.

When the threats are carried out, who will be left hurting at Blackwater Ranch?

Find Remembering the Cowboy on Amazon now!

Made in the USA
Monee, IL
02 August 2022